CHAMPION

CHAMPION

KIMBERLEY ASH

TEA ROSE
PUBLISHING

Dedication

For my mother, who loved horses and posh things

1

Patricia's hat had turned out exactly as ordered: refined on one side, bonkers on the other. To her left, the delicate pink linen swooped down and flared out so that it almost touched her shoulder. To the right, the linen followed the line up, and the space beneath was filled with hundreds of white silk petals resembling Patricia's favourite flower, the peony. Today, despite the horses, she had chosen a simple white dress so that the hat would stand out. As she and her group left the limousine at the entrance to Ascot Racecourse, Patricia felt she was representing her family quite adequately.

"First order of business," she said to Hannah and Sophia, who had come with her, spouses in tow.

"Worship at the altar of your father?" said Hannah. She'd gone with black and white geometric shapes in her hat today, which towered at least a foot above her head.

"I think the worshipping is mutual," said Sophia, in white and lilac. Actual lilacs. "You people sicken me."

Patricia laughed and kissed her cheek (carefully). "I'll find you all before the third race."

"We'll save you some champers," called Sophia as her husband pulled her away. They'd arrived in his family's helicopter, and Hannah's father had provided the limo and clubroom. Patricia was providing the horses.

Her nude stilettos brought her quickly to the parade ring, to the bustle and noise and shouts and occasional whinnies of her father's world. Horseflesh and statistics and feed and jockeys the size of eleven-year-olds who were dwarfed by the creatures they sat on. Patricia stayed on the edge, outside the ring. She was recognized and waved to by many of the other observers. Photographers stepped in and out of pockets of owners and trainers, indistinguishable from each other in grey top hats and morning coats, as they patted necks and gave last-minute advice.

But Gerald, the Earl of Danby, was not there. Nor, as she walked back along the hardpacked Horse Walk, did she see him following behind one of his beloved charges.

"Hello, Monte!" she called up to the jockey on the horse which approached. "How's she feeling today?" She nodded to the lad leading the horse.

The horse Monte rode lifted her perfect head at the sound of her owner's voice. Patricia didn't go to the stables as often as her father, but she knew every one of the horses, and usually had a horsenut or two for them in her pockets. Not to-day, though. Not in this dress.

"Woah, girl," said Monte, pulling the reins lightly so that Crackerjax, a spindly chestnut with soulful brown eyes, couldn't wander out of line towards Patricia. Billy, the lad, waved at her as well.

"She'll be ready to go, Miss," he said. "Bit of a palaver back there, but she's right enough." He stuck his thumb behind him with his free hand.

"Oh, dear. What kind of—" But they were walking past her now.

"You might want to go back there, Miss," Billy said over his shoulder. Monte gave her a chagrined smile over hers.

Patricia waited a second more, watching the beautiful comportment of Gerald's beloved horse. She loved them, too, because it was in her blood, but she didn't live and breathe them the way he did.

Well, she wasn't going to find Gerald on the Horse Walk, obviously. It was too soon before the first race for him to be in the owners' rooms, and as she approached the pre-parade ring and fielded welcoming nods and handshakes from fellow horse-owners, she kept a sharp ear out for his particular sergeant-majorish inflection.

And that of his head trainer.

Patricia sniffed and lifted her chin. Today, she was going to have fun. She was going to drink some champagne, eat a lot of rich food, and give her friends the inside scoop on the horses they should bet on. She was *not* going to let Daniel Stowe and his contemptuous stares get to her.

As she got closer to the pre-parade ring, she heard them. She heard them because they were not with the horses milling about in the ring, but at the edge near the fence. And because one of them was shouting.

"You did it deliberately!" her father's voice yelled. "You kept me out of it!"

Oh, God. Palaver indeed. Patricia picked up her pace.

The crowd parted before her and she saw two of the ubiquitous top hats, very close to each other, one shorter than the other and bristling with anger. "For goodness' sake," she muttered to herself, and hurried over, ducking under the fence and showing her owner's badge to the steward.

The taller hat lifted as its owner raised his head, and Patricia steeled herself against her first look at Daniel in six weeks. With all the preparations under way for the race, and Patricia's own work with the charity, they hadn't crossed paths. Or she'd been grateful to be able to ignore him. One of the two.

He seemed darker, more intense than ever. His close-cut hair at the nape of his neck seemed more severe than normal, his eyes almost black as whatever emotions her father was evoking came through them to her.

Quelling the coltish leaping of her heart, she moved forward. "Father!" she called.

Gerald's furious glare was distracted from his head trainer. "Trish!" he yelled across the field. Damn her heels. She had to mince across the soft turf to get to him. "Daniel took Featherbrain out of the Queen Anne!"

"Yes, yes, Pater, all right, but let's not tell the whole world," she soothed, putting a hand on his grey-wool-clad arm. Gerald came to himself and looked around him at the fascinated crowd. Even the horses being led around the ring seemed to have their ears cocked in her direction.

"Come on," she urged, pulling on his arm. "Let's find a quiet spot."

"Quiet," muttered Gerald, as they walked into the Owners and Trainers building. The men instinctively removed their top hats, and Patricia opened a couple of doors, looking for an empty room. "I'm supposed to be quiet when my reputation is about to get torn to bloody shreds?"

"Featherbrain wasn't ready," Daniel said. He'd fallen into line behind her. She looked around at him and he tipped his top hat at her. "My lady," he added. And it would have been just a normal interaction, if it hadn't been for the mocking smile that tugged up the corner of his mouth.

"Knock it off, Daniel," she said, low enough that her father wouldn't hear under his muttering.

"Not a phrase I've heard you use before," he said, his voice low. "Too long in New York buying handbags, milady?"

Patricia scowled at him and opened another door. This room was empty, so she shoved the two of them in.

"Trish!" squawked Gerald. "This is the ladies'!"

"It's empty, and that's all I care about." She closed the door and leaned against it. "Now what on earth is going on?"

Gerald had gone even redder with his new surroundings, and he was already apoplectic. The reminder of his grievance turned him almost purple. "Bloody fool scratched her without a word! I've been talking her up all afternoon!"

"I tried to contact you," Daniel said. Without his hat, his features settled into the man she'd known: keen eyes that saw every detail, hair cut the requisite short back and sides without care to how the top fell over his forehead. Sharp cheekbones that went with his spare frame, showing that he had never been able to move far beyond the Spartan diet of an aspiring jockey.

Unfortunately for Daniel, when he was fifteen he'd had a growth spurt that put him over five feet nine and killed his chances of ever riding his beloved charges. Gerald had kept him on though, impressed by his knowledge and his interest in all the facets of stock management. Ten years later, he'd been made a trainer. Five years after that, he ran the stable.

And didn't speak to Patricia except to goad her.

"I've been out!" Gerald puffed.

"Where's your mobile, Dad?" Patricia asked.

Gerald humphed. "In one of the cars, I expect." He never could remember to keep it on him, no matter how useful everyone told him it was.

"Then you can't shout at Daniel for—"

Daniel's eyes swiveled to hers, eyebrows raised as she went to defend him. But Gerald interrupted.

"Don't tell me what I can't do, young lady! They are *my horses!* He should have driven down early! He scratched her yesterday! Plenty of time!"

Daniel leaned against the wall, folding his arms. "You would have tried to talk me out of it."

"Ha! You see! He did it deliberately!" Gerald stuck a finger in his direction.

"She's not ready," Daniel patiently repeated. "I've been watching her at morning gallops all week. She tired too easily. The lads said the same—"

"I've watched her too! She's perfectly all right! You think I don't know my own horses?"

Daniel didn't say anything, but whatever was in his eyes sent Gerald over the edge. Instead of shouting, his face twisted.

"Just you remember, my lad," he said, his finger an inch from Daniel's face. "Just you remember where you came from, and who brought you here. Sometimes you forget your place."

"Daddy!" Patricia was horrified. Her father was never crass. "Apologize!"

"Get away from the door, my girl, or I won't be responsible." Gerald squared on to her. "I've turned you over my knee before and I can do it again."

"All right, all right, for heaven's sake." She moved away from the door and Gerald wrenched it open, banging it with his hat in his hurry to leave.

They heard his steps echo down the hallway towards the owners' and trainers' room. Patricia wanted to go after him, make him come back and take back his words.

"Forget it," Daniel said behind her.

His Yorkshire accent made her close her eyes. Not that his accent pointed him out as not one of her class; Lord Clarendon's family had come over with William the Conqueror, and his accent was thicker than moor fog. But in this case it didn't help.

"He didn't mean that," she said, hugging the door to her, not turning around.

Daniel paused for too long before she heard, "No."

That made her face him. His face was as familiar to her as the view from her bedroom window, where she'd slept for all her twenty-five years, even though she hadn't been this close to him in months. Even though when she was close to him, there was usually a horse between them. A horse, and their history: their closeness, and their estrangement.

"I mean it," she said now, her voice low. "You're very important to us—to the stable." No, she wasn't going to back down, not this time, not when Gerald had just said what he had. "No. To us. Dad knows that."

Daniel had never been much of a talker. In the old days, she'd found his presence peaceful. They'd cleaned tack together, or read racing forms and dreamed of someday producing their own winners. They'd seen foals born and venerated old stallions die, and either way, Daniel had hardly spoken.

For a very short few hours, she'd had him. But then she'd gone away to university, and she'd lost him.

"It's all right, Lady Patricia," he said.

"Damn you," she snapped. He'd never once used her title, until she'd come back from uni that first Christmas. "Fine, Daniel, if that's the way you want it." She pointed to the grey top hat he jogged loosely in one hand, the only sign he gave that he was also upset. "Want to tip that hat at me again while you're at it?"

"I just want to do my job, milady," he drawled.

What an idiot she'd been, to try and comfort him. He was as cold as the tiled wall behind him.

Patricia got the door the rest of the way open and walked out, her heels tapping out her anger as she put distance between them. That anger carried her all the way from the O&T rooms, through the pre-parade ring and horse walk, through the other racegoers and up to the club room Hannah had booked. Only when she was inside it, with the soothing buzz of talk from her friends and a breeze from the open windows surrounding her, did she take a deep breath and realize she had a blister on both heels. "Shit," she groaned, falling into a chair next to Sophia.

"There you are!"

"What on earth happened?"

"You look absolutely spent!" Patricia's friends made it easy for her to wave away the whole incident with a laugh and a request for a glass of champagne.

"Did I miss the race?" she asked.

"I'm afraid so," said Hannah. "Crackerjax came third."

"Oh, good for her." *Daniel will be pleased with that*, she thought at once, then chided herself and took a deep drink of bubbles.

"All right, dear, we've got all afternoon," said Howard, Viscount Alexander, Sophia's husband.

Patricia laughed. "You're so right, Alex. Plenty of time for you to make me up a plate." She beamed at him and Alex dutifully trotted off to serve her.

She hadn't eaten much of the salmon toast and scotch quail eggs with which Alex had filled her plate before they were called to the balcony to watch the fourth race. "Look at Covendish go," she murmured to Sophia next to her, drawing her attention to the colt, in her father's colours of green and orange harlequin, who was prancing to his gate.

"Trish, dear, you're supposed to have told me this a few minutes ago, so we could have put some money on him," Sophia chided. "Alex, darling?" She waggled her glass at him.

"Pimm's?" he asked, and when she nodded, left them again.

"You have him so well-trained," Patricia commented.

"So do you," answered Hannah, who was at the railing. Her husband, Padraig—pronounced Porrig, no title—was new and so never far from her side.

"I didn't want him to hear me ask you about Daniel. Por, lovey, don't listen," Sophia called over Hannah's head.

"This might come as a shock to you ladies, but I want to watch the race," Padraig answered in his Galway brogue. The starting gun went off and he turned away.

"Right," said Sophia. Behind her, Hannah nodded encouragingly at Patricia. "So did you see Daniel?"

Patricia lifted her glass up near her face so she could point at her eyes. "See this? This is me rolling my eyes. Look, watch them roll."

"Don't fob us off," begged Hannah. "Was he with your father?"

"Was he wearing his morning suit?" said Sophia.

"Of course he was," Hannah said. "He has to."

"Does he look as hot as ever?"

"Sophie!"

"What? I just think he scrubs up nice, that's all."

"He's the head trainer, not the boy who shovels the dung."

"You fancied him even when he was, though."

"I did not!" But she could feel herself blushing.

She hadn't "fancied" him. That implied a mere physical reaction, an admiration of eyes or mouth or haircut, an hour spent standing in a barn, forking out hay instead of writing her essay on Montesquieu's *Lettres Persanes* because Daniel had been there too.

Okay, she had done that.

But her connection with Daniel had been bone deep almost before she'd known what "fancying" was. He'd been a part of her life the way her land was, the way the pile of Danby Hall that sat overlooking it and the moors to the west was.

She stared out as the horses disappeared round the bend, not seeing them. Then she sniffed and lifted her chin, her failsafe for stopping her from thinking about him that way.

"Darling Hannah," she smiled, "just because you found your rustic charmer, doesn't mean I need one. Let's watch Covendish win."

They obeyed her, but then they heard a voice. "Someone's mobile's ringing."

The ladies had all left their clutches in the clubroom. So Covendish went around the far curve of the course unobserved by Patricia's party. Hannah spilled her champagne and Sophia never got her Pimm's.

When they got into the room, Daniel was there.

"Tricia," he said.

He'd called her by her name. His name for her. Fear slammed into her chest. "God. What?"

The ringtone was hers, but it stopped before Daniel spoke again.

"Your father." He swallowed, and now that she wasn't blinded by the dark room after the brightness of the course outside, she saw that he was as white as a sheet.

Patricia's legs shook, but she remained standing. Lifted her chin.

"What is it?" asked Alex. "Come on, Daniel."

They all knew him from their visits to the stables with her.

Daniel was still looking at Patricia. "You'd better come," he said.

"You're scaring me, Daniel," she said. Her voice didn't shake, thank God.

"Yes." Now his eyes flicked to Alex and the rest of them. "You might want to come too, my lord."

Sophia and Hannah surged forward, each linking their arms through Patricia's. Alex wordlessly took the drink she was still holding and put it to one side for her, before following the ladies out of the room. As she left, Patricia heard her phone ring again.

Back down the stairs, through the crowd, into the parade ring, the horsewalk, the pre-parade ring where she'd seen Gerald shout, into the passageway where she'd pushed him into the ladies' loo, what seemed like hours ago. Up more stairs. Patricia felt her jaw get stiffer and stiffer with each step.

They'd put him in an anteroom to the side of the main lounge, a quiet room for talking that was now silent as the... Well.

"Patricia, darling," said a voice. Another owner. Hamid Al-Sayad, a good friend of Gerald's, almost an uncle to her. He swam in her peripheral vision, his cufflinks alone worth Gerald's entire outfit. "He said he didn't feel well."

Didn't feel well. That's an understatement. The words were hollow in her mind. Dimly she heard Hannah and Sophia, sniffing back tears next to her.

A St. John's Ambulance man was in a uniform to her right. "It was very quick, miss," he said, in what should have been a soothing tone. But it grated on her, burrowed into her stunned mind the way nothing else had.

Gerald was still red in the face, though not as much as when she'd last seen him. His hair was smoothed back from his face, but his coat was off and his tie and shirt had been loosened.

"Did..." she said. In the ten minutes since she'd last spoken, her throat had dried up. "Did someone try to—" *If it was quick, why did they bother giving him CPR?*

There was a silence, then a throat cleared, like she wanted to make hers do, only she couldn't work the muscles. "I did."

Patricia turned, breaking away from Hannah and Sophia. Daniel was in the doorway. Now she saw that he was also disheveled: his own shirt and tie undone, his hat long gone, his hair messy and falling into his eyes. *Breaking the rules. I'm surprised they let him walk around like that.*

It came to her in a rush: the argument, Gerald's face, his heart. Daniel's stubbornness, the insult. Patricia let out a sound she'd only heard animals in pain give and launched herself at him, knocking him to the floor, which kept him where she could hit him. "You!" she was screaming, and she couldn't seem to stop. "You did this! You!"

She struck every inch of him she could reach before they pulled her off him, and she was still screaming and groaning when Alex stepped forward and gave her a gentle shake.

Her cries cut off, leaving an echo in the small room and the foyer outside. "Come on, old girl," Alex said, not the servant to his wife any more, but the heir to half of Sussex that he'd been born to. "That's right." And this time her legs did buckle, and she slipped to the floor and her friends' arms went around her, and she closed her eyes against Daniel's figure, still prone where she'd left him, refusing offers of help to stand.

2

The funeral itself was tasteful and small, but the entire village turned out to send the Earl of Danby off. The black carriage and horses were worth a pause in the street as they clattered by, and it had been made known that all were welcome at Danby Hall, to toast Gerald with some of the contents of his own wine cellar.

Patricia was happy the village was there, because when they were, she didn't have to think. She went into her social mode, smiling and shaking hands, saying the inane things people expected, asking the villagers about their lives, laughing politely at stories of her father, half-listening, not letting them hit the black rock that sat in her heart.

She stood next to her brother most of the afternoon. Viscount Worcester, now the new Earl of Danby, had long red hair tied back for the occasion with a thick strip of leather that coiled down his back like a snake. She'd warned him on pain of death ("bad choice of words, old thing," he'd said over the phone) to stop at Norton and Sons and pick up a black suit. "I already called them and they're making it up to your measurements," she'd told him.

"Yes, about that…" he'd said, and she saw what he'd meant when he'd walked down to breakfast and his trousers had nearly fallen down.

"Didn't you try it on?" she'd moaned as she rang for Mrs. Gennaro and a needle.

"You only said to pick it up," he'd pointed out, and then, "Ah, eggs. Can't beat the nosh here, that's one thing. Only so many kilos a man can keep on with a diet of chicken feet and rice."

Patricia suppressed a shudder now, remembering. Her little brother had never fit in with the world he'd been born to. He and Gerald had clashed so often it had been a relief, really, when James had found a vocation in rural China and left them. Patricia had to admit, even with the present occasion and his loss of weight, James looked happy.

Well, she'd been happy too. She'd been fulfilled, and she'd been useful. Now she'd have to... what? What would *James* have to do? He was a peer of the realm now, God help him. Gerald's robes were upstairs, waiting for the first day of Parliament. Somehow she couldn't see James ever putting them on. She imagined him, showing up in the House of Lords, that red snake of hair down his back, and Black Rod shutting the door in *his* face. Patricia let out a snort.

"Oh, I'm so sorry," she said to Countess Sterling, to whom she'd been politely nodding as the old lady talked. "Something stuck in my throat."

"Trish, love," said Viscount Alexander over Countess Sterling's head. "Hello, Aunt," he added, smoothly taking his aunt's hand, kissing her cheek and inserting himself where she'd been standing. "Want me to start shooing?" he said to Patricia.

She looked at the slim gold watch on her wrist. It had been her mother's, as was the black 1950s-style dress she wore, complete with black petticoats and flared skirt, and the pearls at her neck. Her own hair, a lighter red than James', was partly covered with a simple band and veil. The one and only occasion she'd given herself to cry was when she'd taken the dress out of the wardrobe in her mother's room.

"No, thanks, Alex," she said. "Let's give them a few more minutes to poke around."

There was no acerbity in her voice. She loved her home, knew the provenance of every piece of furniture, the name of every one of the portraits on the walls. She knew how many man hours it took to vacuum every carpet and change every bed in the Hall, how much she should budget for a dinner for forty, and which maid was sleeping with the butler (Jessica, and Patricia had high hopes for her and DaShawn). Each summer, the family opened the house to visitors and hired docents to give tours, but an event like this gave the surrounding villagers a chance to admire—or condemn—her lifestyle for free, and she didn't begrudge it them.

"I think that man in the corner eating all the strawberries wants to talk to you."

She hit his arm. "Alex. That's Daddy's solicitor. I'm sure he wants to set up an appointment to go over the estate."

"Well, your greenhouses will be stripped of berries for the summer if you don't get over there."

Grateful for the gentle laugh he induced, Patricia went over to the man. "Mr. Fisher?"

"Lady Patricia," he replied, hastily wiping his hand on a napkin. "Might I say how sorry I am?"

"Thank you," she said with the slight smile her mouth was stuck in today. "I wanted to thank you for your consideration over the last few days."

"Not at all. But I wondered if I might be able to meet with you both for a few minutes," he said, with a nod to where James stood, a scarecrow among mannequins. "While your brother is still in the country?"

Patricia was tired. She'd been in heels all day and her back hurt. She wanted to deal with the weight of the responsibility that was to fall to her tomorrow. But of course she didn't say any of that. "Of course," she said, smiling at his joke. Everyone knew James would be gone soon, even though a large part of her wanted to fall on his neck and beg him to stay, to help her share the burden. Who else did she have?

"Would Mr. Stowe be able to join us?" asked Mr. Fisher.

"Daniel?" She'd been so determined to put him out of her mind that the mention of his name shocked her. He was at the house, she knew. He would have seen to the horses this morning and then joined the crowd. Gerald would not have been surprised if he'd been at the funeral. But Patricia had drawn the line. She was still too angry.

"Yes. Would he be able to join us, do you think?"

"Is he in the will?" She hadn't looked for it yet, had used the last five days to organize the funeral and nothing else.

"Lord Danby left instructions," was Mr. Fisher's cryptic reply.

"Oh, right." Patricia looked around her, non-plussed. And she was even more non-plussed when she found Daniel immediately, as if he'd been waiting near her all afternoon. He was twenty feet away, in a knot of her father's friends and other trainers, but he met her eyes almost as soon as she looked at him.

Well, she wasn't about to show him what she thought of him in front of them. Excusing herself from the solicitor, she walked over.

She began by greeting everyone but Daniel, enjoying the brief respite their welcome and condolences gave her. However, she couldn't put it off forever. "Daniel," she said, and tried not to tingle at the dark look he was giving her. "A moment of your time, if you would."

"Certainly, my lady," he answered. Did everyone else hear how he said that? Was it just her? Anyway, no one reacted and she didn't think her cheeks had heated enough that they'd notice.

They stepped away from the group. "Pater's solicitor would like to talk to us," she said without preamble.

Daniel looked as surprised as she felt. "Me?"

"And me. And James."

Daniel frowned, but he followed her as she scooped up James and led the three men out of the public areas and through a corridor to her father's study. She locked the door behind them.

The last time I locked Daniel in a room like this, Dad died.

The study didn't help, being everything that was Gerald. The oldest furniture in the house, dating from the seventeenth century, pure walnut and heavy as hell. Curtains his grandfather had put up and which took the servants a week to dust. Pictures of horses on every inch of wall and most of the bookshelves. The room even looked down the hill towards the stables. And it smelled of leather and scotch and his cologne, which he'd had made especially in Paris.

Patricia felt her throat begin to close, and concentrated on how much of a sendoff she would be giving his valet when he officially retired next week.

Mr. Fisher had a briefcase she hadn't noticed before. It must have been behind him while he gorged on strawberries. He pulled three envelopes from it and handed one to each of them.

"There you are," he said, closing the briefcase with that satisfying *chunk* all briefcases have. "Thank you very much. If you have any concerns, please do contact me."

All three of them stared at the papers in their hands. "Aren't you going to read it out loud?" said James, looking lost.

Mr. Fisher chuckled. "No, my lord." James winced a little. He'd been away so long, he'd forgotten his title, Patricia realized. "That's just in the films. It's all quite straightforward. Lady Patricia, you'll be sure to contact me as soon as you wish, to transfer powers of attorney and that sort of thing."

"Yes," said Patricia faintly, still holding the envelope in front of her. So much for dramatic revelations and outbursts barely held in in front of the lawyers. "Thank you."

"Not at all. I'll show myself out." And he did.

James broke the silence first. "Daniel, I haven't had a chance to talk to you." He put down the will and shook the smaller man's hand. "Bugger of a thing."

"Yes," said Daniel.

"You were with him, I heard? They said you did CPR?"

She thought perhaps Daniel was studiously not looking at her. "Yes. I tried."

"Well, thank you, old man." James shook his hand again. "He loved you, you know. Like you were another son."

She did love James so much. When he'd shed the aristocracy he'd also shed any jealousy toward anyone his father approved of more than him.

Daniel looked down, opened his mouth and closed it again. *God, no. If he starts crying I will not be able to stop myself. And I will not feel sorry for him.*

"Let's read them, shall we?" she said. Her voice was harsh after James' gentle tones.

"Oh, yes, that would be the thing, I suppose," said James, and they slit open their envelopes.

James' equanimity didn't last long. "But I don't want it!" he exclaimed after a moment.

Patricia had known something like this would happen. "You're the earl now, Jamie. All this," she waved at the room, the house, the acres, "is yours."

"Almost all," commented Daniel.

"He should have given *all* of it to you!" James cried. "Not just the horses!"

"He can't, you loony. That's what I'm trying to tell you. You're the boy. You're the earl. It's yours."

"That's absolutely ridiculous. I'm leaving tomorrow."

Patricia fiddled with the corner of her copy. "Jamie, dear, would it really be so bad if you stayed? You have plenty of countryside here to... to do whatever you want with. Within reason. People who rely on the estate. We have several conservation projects—"

"No," James stressed, his eyes wide, their whites showing how tanned his skin was. "I'm sorry, Trish, but I just can't. They need me out there. I'm running a school. You know what the orphans in that district would do if I didn't keep it going?"

"I know how much it costs, yes." It cost less than the feed for five horses a year. Most of the money came from James' allowance. The few occasions that brought him back to England were when he had to fundraise for the rest.

"Not the money." James began moving around the room, pulling his tie off and unbuttoning his top button at the same time. "They need *me*. They're my kids."

Patricia didn't let her shoulders slump, because Daniel was there, but she could almost hear the door slam closed on her vain hope that James would help her. "All right, Jamie. I know you have to go back. We just do like seeing you here as well."

He kissed her cheek. "You're not so bad yourself, old thing," he said warmly. "I tell my kids about my beautiful sister with hair the colour of... chicken feathers."

Patricia punched him and he hugged her and made for the door. "You've read it all already?" she said.

He shrugged. "You'll tell me if there's anything else. I expect I'll have some papers to sign over at Mr. Fisher's soon." And he was gone.

Leaving Patricia and Daniel alone again.

She set her face in lines of dislike, as she'd promised herself she would if she saw him today. But the pain on Daniel's face as he looked up from the will nearly undid her. He hadn't taken part in her and James' conversation, but kept his head bent over his copy of the will. Now she saw that there were two pieces of paper in his hand.

"He left me another letter," he said, his voice tight.

"Oh?" She hoped she sounded indifferent. "What does it say?"

"I think you have one too," was his answer.

Patricia looked, and there was.

Trish, my darling girl, she read, and she was unprepared for the emotion that pushed at her throat and eyes, hearing Gerald's voice in the words.

I hope I've been able to teach you everything I know about the house, and the role, and most especially the horses. I hope you're reading this in your late seventies, and I went out at a hundred and ten, riding every morning to the end. But those quacks at Guy's have told me that's not likely. The old ticker's not what she was, my darling, and I'm afraid you'll be reading this sooner rather than later.

We've been a great team, you and I. But we've had a partner in all that success. If you haven't chucked him out yet for whatever it is he did, or if he's forgiven you for whatever it was you did (more likely, I'm afraid, old girl; you are rather terrifying sometimes) I want you to keep Daniel on. He's a good lad. He loves the land as much as you do, and the horses more so.

You're going to hit a bugger of a tax bill now—something I meant to deal with someday. You might have to let some of the horses go. If he's still around, have Daniel choose which ones. You're a sentimental creature under it all, and he's more clearheaded about these things.

All right, that's all. I'm more proud of you every day you're by my side. Don't be sad when you read this, old girl. I'll be with your mother, and I've waited a long time for that.

Your loving Pater

The page was smudged with tears and Patricia had sunk onto a chair before she'd finished reading. She covered her face with one hand, the paper crushed, forgotten, in the other, as she tried to control her sobs.

"Tricia," Daniel said softly.

"Don't talk to me!" she cried. "If it weren't for you... if not for you and bloody Featherbrain!"

"I know it. I—"

"I didn't even get to say goodbye to him! He didn't even look at me and then he was *gone* and *you did that!*"

"Tricia," he said again.

He was in front of her, crouched to her level, taking the hand that held the letter. She wanted to pull away, but she wanted comfort as well. Her grief outweighed her anger. She let his hand stay.

"Don't look at me," she whispered, still covering her face.

"Why do the upper classes always treat displays of emotion as if they were attacks of herpes?" he said with amusement.

"Shut up," she said, but it was a sob and when he put his arms around her she didn't protest, but cried into his shoulder, and Daniel rubbed her back and her hair and murmured, "There, lass," and for those few seconds, Patricia was supported.

She became aware of his scent, of the horses that never quite left him, the leather and soap and hay that made up his life, that were such a part of hers even though she wasn't with them every day. And his skin, that was warm and damp with her tears, his hard chest under her hand, and the flutter that took over her heart now that the burst of crying was over. She pulled away.

But that was a mistake, because now she was inches from his face, and those dark eyes, that had seen all of her from the very beginning, were boring into her, and his lips were right there, and all she had to do was—

"What did it say?" he asked. "The letter?"

Some small part of her still wanted to keep to itself. "What did yours say?" she answered.

"That he was going to ask you to keep me on. That we should work out our differences. For the horses." He smiled at her, but then sobered. "Trish, if I could have saved him..."

"No," she said, accepting it herself now that she had Gerald's own admission. "He knew his heart was worse than he'd told me."

"I know. That's why I didn't tell him—"

Patricia backed up another inch. "What do you mean, you know?"

The truth was written across his face. "He made me swear—"

"You knew he was this ill? And you didn't tell me?" She threw his hands back at him. Where before she'd felt a reassuring warmth at his proximity, now Patricia knew only cold.

"Tricia, he told me not to."

"And you listened to him? Rather than thinking of—of me?" Her voice matched the ice in her veins.

"I've done nothing but—"

Patricia stood, cutting off his words. Lifted her chin and wiped the tears on her cheeks. Checked her veil, pulled it a little farther over one eye. "I have to get back to the mourners."

Daniel stood as well. "Tricia, will you—"

"You'll be at morning exercises tomorrow? Good. I don't want anyone to think anything has changed." Her eyes met his at the last word. "Because nothing has."

A muscle visibly clenched in Daniel's jaw. "Ever the lady," he bit out. "Always making things fit the story you want to believe, right? All right, then." He went to the door and pulled it open. "I'll be at my post in the morning as usual, *my lady*," he said, with all the offence he could fit into the phrase. He turned his back on her and left the room.

He'd left his letter and copy of the will on the desk. Patricia looked down at it. The ringing betrayal that he had known Gerald was ill and hadn't told her was still clanging in her ears. She opened the letter.

Daniel,

I'm instructing Trish to keep you on as head trainer. If she hasn't pissed you off too much in between me writing this and me dying (funny, I don't feel like I am), help her. She needs you more than she'll ever admit.

Hamid will try and poach you. If you go, I'll understand, but I hope you'll stay.

I've been privileged to know you. They used to say men like you couldn't be found in the lower classes, without a war to temper them. But you are every bit the son I've wanted, and I say that without removing one iota of my love for James. I can't leave you the stable, and he doesn't want it. So be there for Trish. Don't let her push you away.

Danby

She shouldn't have read it. She was stuck with him; every word that Gerald had written was a tie to hold Daniel to the stable and through it, to her. Her father didn't have to say those things about Patricia needing him, because she didn't. The horses did.

She would never forgive Daniel for respecting her father's wishes over what would obviously have been her own. She might have to work with him, but she would never again get as close to him as she'd been today. Any intimacy they'd ever shared was far in the past. The future was the estate.

3

Hamid, her father's friend, put his head around the study door while Daniel's letter was still in her hand. "Oh, good," he said. "You're alone."

Given Gerald's letters, she'd expected Hamid would visit soon. But perhaps he could have waited until the guests had gone. "Yes," she said, folding the letter and leaving it on the desk. "Come in, Hamid."

Hamid's black suit was impeccable and he entered the room with all due respect to Gerald. So as not to make him feel like a client, Patricia took one of the armchairs in front of the fire and motioned Hamid to take the other. She knew better than to offer him a drink, but she said, "Would you like some tea?"

Hamid smiled. "There is more tea available out there than at your..." He seemed to grope for a name. "...Women's Institute meetings. I am not here as your guest, Patricia, but as a friend."

Oh, good, more grand advice. Hamid had probably known about Gerald's illness as well, but with him it was less of a betrayal. She would expect Gerald to tell his friend, but not his... employee.

Daniel's been more than an employee for fifteen years and you know it.

Patricia tried to refocus on Hamid. This day was interminable. "Of course you're a friend, Hamid. We've relied on your good sense for years. I know my father cared about you very much."

Hamid bowed his head. "I appreciate that, Patricia. I hope he knew that his friendship meant a great deal to me as well. The entire racing industry will miss his presence, but I will miss... I will miss riding out with him, watching morning exercises and comparing bloodstock."

An awkward pause followed, while Patricia smiled and swallowed and thought *don't you dare cry.*

"Ah," Hamid went on. "I've been too emotional. I apologize. Let's get back to business."

Now? Couldn't she have one day before she had to think about the estate?

"My dearest Patricia, you are going to have to find a husband."

That snapped her eyes to his. Patricia felt her mouth drop open. If she'd been American, she might have said, "Excuse me?"

Hamid put out a hand and gave her knee a paternal pat. "I am sorry to have to bring it up. I would like to tell you that I will make all your problems go away. I promised Gerald I would watch out for you, but your inheritance laws leave my hands tied in many ways."

"I don't expect you to—" she began, but he held up his hand, richly endowed with gold rings.

"I cannot help the fact that your brother has inherited the entire estate."

"Not the horses."

"Ah!" Hamid looked pleased. "So he did change his will. I am glad for you."

"But we'll probably have to sell them to pay the inheritance taxes."

Hamid looked out of the window, down the lawn towards the stables. "This would be a tragedy."

"Less of a tragedy than losing the estate."

His dark eyes came back to hers. "Your father has been—forgive me, had been—breeding that line for forty years. You would not let the Danby name fall into legend?"

Patricia found that her knee wanted to jiggle. She clamped both knees together, her feet demurely tucked to one side under the enormous chair. "I don't know what I'm going to do yet, Hamid. I only just read the will. But I'm not ruling anything out at this point."

Hamid nodded and rubbed his chin. "You are right. This is conjecture. But, to get back to where I began, the title is not conjecture. Your brother has the land, the house, the earldom. Everything."

"Yes." A tiny stab of pain smote her at the thought; at the knowledge that she had always loved the land and everything on it more than James and that her dedication was being swept aside by a centuries-old law. But she pushed away the pain. What was the point in indulging it?

Things were the way they were. She was in the house now. That had to be good enough.

"And if he ever gets married, his wife will—forgive me—take your place."

Patricia's hands were clutched together in her lap. Why was he bringing her this today? "If he marries." She went for amusement. "You know Jamie, Hamid. He'll never settle down for long enough to get married. And if he does, he won't come here."

"He might." Hamid shifted to the front of his seat. "He might, my dear, and that is why I must advise you to get married as quickly as possible and leave this place to him and the family he will—"

"*Leave?*" Patricia gave up her attempts to control her shaking limbs. She stood up. "I can't *leave*. There's no one else to run the estate."

"Sell it."

"*Hamid!*"

"I am sorry," he said again. "I am sorry to be so blunt. But you cannot allow yourself to become so attached to this place when you will have to leave it one way or the other, and soon. Do you really think that James will *never* find a woman who will want to come back to the thousand acres he just happens to own in the most beautiful part of England?"

"I—he—"

"I know. He is committed to his village and his school. But he is young, and many things will change. And you need to change too."

Patricia put some starch into her voice. "I didn't realize I was defective the way I am."

To his credit, Hamid didn't take the bait, but merely smiled in that serene way he had. "You are perfect the way you are, Patricia, but your way is this life." He waved his hand around the luxuriously scruffy room. "This world. Your great-grandmother's legacy. The children you went to school with. Your feel for the land and your responsibility to the people who work on it."

Patricia winced inwardly. The idea of *noblesse oblige* had died with the First World War, but there was no denying that as their employer and their landlord, she had a lot more involvement in her employees' lives than usual.

"Your respect for history," Hamid continued. "What I am trying to say is that you will not be able to give this up and move to a flat in London if and when James comes home with a bride."

How did he know that? She'd barely formed the words in her own mind. Hadn't wanted to think about ever needing to leave Danby. Whenever her thoughts strayed in that direction, for some reason Daniel was always standing there, and as she shied away from him, so she didn't let herself think about the future. In any case, the future had always included Gerald.

"So your solution is that I marry?" she tried to say with some amusement. "That doesn't keep me at Danby."

"No. But you need a house similar to this, with a life similar to this. And there are plenty of estates crying out for your skills. And men who would appreciate the privilege of marrying you."

He inclined his head in respect, but his words still hurt. Marrying for land. For money. She was in a Jane Austen novel.

And what about love? she wanted to shout. *What about desire? What about a man who loves the land like I do, who grew up here with me? Who would help me, not hire me?*

Her lips tightened. She didn't think Hamid could read her. She'd been well brought up in that way. Gerald's red face and choleric nature had been an anomaly in their circles. Perhaps that was why Hamid had liked him so much. Gerald hadn't had a stiff upper lip.

"That is all I wanted to say," Hamid went on. "I have to leave the country for a week or I wouldn't have mentioned it today." He stood; Patricia automatically rose with him. "You are comporting yourself admirably, my dear, and the service was everything Gerald would have wished. He would be proud of you."

Patricia tightened her lips further. Too many emotions to squash down. Too much. She shook her head.

Hamid understood. He patted her arm and showed himself out of Gerald's study.

Patricia touched the lampshade that stood closest to her. It was dark green and shaded a brass light that had been bought when Gerald's father was a boy. He'd told Patricia of the excitement when the house had finally been wired for electricity. The servants dutifully dusted the shade and its bronze-coloured tassels, as if Gerald would at any moment walk up to it and turn it on.

Her shoulders shook before she could stop them. Her legs folded her back into the wingchair. She gripped the worn red leather of the armrest hard while another sob escaped her.

But there were the guests. And her ravaged makeup. And they might be running low on canapes. People might be leaving and if she wasn't there to say goodbye, they would talk about it.

She sniffed, forced strength into her limbs, pressed a finger to the skin below her eyes. Found a mirror Gerald kept near his desk and checked her makeup. Put on the mantle she was born to, and went back to the funeral.

4

The interminable afternoon ended and Patricia and Jamie were left alone in the house (not counting twelve servants). True to his word, Jamie left the next morning. Though she suspected he was going to be spending a few days in London with a girl he had a friends-with-benefits arrangement with, she didn't challenge him.

When he had his backpack in the boot of the car and Everett, the driver, was waiting patiently to close his door, Jamie hugged her to his spare frame. "Take care of yourself, old girl," he said.

There was no one else left to call her that. Patricia smiled and swallowed down a threat of tears. "Be careful," she said into his shoulder. Then, before she could stop herself, she added, "And do come back soon."

If she'd expected any sense of fraternal duty suddenly to appear in Jamie's pale blue eyes, she was disappointed. "You'll be fine," he said, pulling her away to give her his usual carefree grin. "You were born to this, Trish. Enjoy it."

And he was gone, the sand-coloured gravel crunching under the car's wheels, and the house's curator wanted to meet with her about some damage the guests had done yesterday, and the bank wanted her to sign some papers, and Gerald had never allowed the housekeeper to replace the curtains in the south gallery and they were about to fall off their rails, and Mrs. Gennaro wanted to go over the meals for the week, and Patricia's assistant had arrived and was patiently waiting for her at the door. And so Patricia put on the mantle and stepped into her life.

One blessing of all the extra duties she now had to fulfil was that she could easily find an excuse to avoid the stables. She knew Daniel was there, half a mile down the hill, making the stables run like the proverbial clockwork, putting money in the Danby coffers and asking very little in return. Gerald's horses—her horses now, she supposed—were running at Epsom and Kempton Park this week, but she was not about to talk to Daniel about their chances, or even about their feed. She was relieved to see the charge on the corporate credit card for his hotel room.

Gerald had left him fifty thousand pounds. Rather, he'd given him fifty thousand, several years ago, with the understanding that the gift reduced the estate and so saved on inheritance tax. The will instructed Patricia to give ten percent of the estate to her charity and James' orphanage, which also reduced the tax bill, and there were substantial debts, as in any large business. But the bill still ran into the millions, she had six months to start paying it, and there was only one way to do so.

When Daniel got back from Kempton Park a few days later, Patricia was waiting in the yard. He nodded to her as he got out of the trailer, but gave her no more attention, instead instructing the lads on getting the horses settled into their stalls.

But when he began to follow them to the barn, she called out. "Daniel? Do you have a minute?"

He paused, then turned on his heel and walked back to her. "Certainly, my lady."

She narrowed her eyes at him, but his face was guileless. As it should be in front of the other employees. "Might we go into your office?" she asked.

He nodded and indicated that she go in front of him. Patricia wanted to scream at him, but she also didn't want people to start talking about them.

Daniel had taken over this office a year ago and as far as Patricia could see, had made no changes to it whatsoever. The walls were lined with bloodstock books and veterinary journals and feed catalogs and so much paper Patricia had trouble remembering what century she was in. The desk was the same battered old chipboard that Daniel's predecessor had used. One corner was damaged, the woodchips inside sprinkled on the faded carpet below.

The only difference was what was on the desk. Patricia herself had stepped in when Daniel had asked Gerald for a computer. The antiquated box that Sid Hislop had used was barely even worthy of the term. Now that Daniel had the correct equipment (over Gerald's protests, but it was one of the times when Patricia allowed herself to get involved, and he could never overrule her), the rest of the desk was almost bare. Only a telephone and a notepad stood ready.

Daniel put his overnight bag on the floor near the bookshelves and began to pull items out of a large saddlebag: three notebooks, a tablet with an industrial-strength case, his cellphone which was almost as big as the tablet and similarly protected, and lastly, hanging limply in his hand after all the hard-edged technology, a black armband.

It wasn't expected of him. He'd been out in public before now and one wearing was usually enough. But he'd taken it to Kempton Park. He wasn't letting Gerald's memory fade for a while yet.

The sight of the armband softened Patricia's resolution to be as formal with him as possible. "Thank you for that," she said, nodding at it. "Gerald liked a bit of ceremony."

"I wasn't the only one," he answered. He put the armband in a top drawer. "I have a long list of people who sent you their... condolences."

Sent you their love, was what he was going to say. But that was a very fraught word between them, and he'd obviously felt it beyond him.

Time to return to safe topics. "How did they run?" she asked.

"Mostly as expected. Eddie Bailey buggered up the start of the Padgett and Gazillion couldn't make it up, but otherwise they did well."

"What will you do about Eddie?"

Daniel took off his beaten-up waxed jacket—a mirror of the one Patricia had worn down to the stables—and stepped around her to hang it on a hook by the door. This brought him close to her.

Patricia wanted to shift her feet to give him room, really she did, but she couldn't move. A part of her that had never learned wanted to get close to him whenever the opportunity arose.

He was dressed in heavy canvas khakis, a blue collared shirt and a chunky navy fisherman's sweater with a shawl collar. Incongruously, on his feet he wore slim ankle boots, made to ride delicate racehorses.

"Gave him a bollocking." His hair was messy from the flat cap he'd hung up when they'd walked in, and now that she was looking at him, standing inches from him, *breathing* with him, he put up a hand to smooth down his cowlick. But had he really noticed? He was speaking quite normally. "He's lost his chance at the next three races. If he learns after that, good. Otherwise, he's out."

He hadn't moved away. Perhaps he wanted her to know that he was unaffected by her. That he had never been affected by her. Apart from that one night...

"Uh," she said past the lump in her throat. "Do you think he'll learn?"

They were the same height, so when he looked at her he really *looked* at her. Patricia forgot what she'd asked.

"Aye," he said. "He's careless but he loves the horses. He'll work it out."

"Good." It was barely a squeak.

His dark eyes kept hers captive for a while longer. "Y'alright, are ya?" he said at last. His Yorkshire rarely came on this strong. Then again, he was in his domain, one Patricia had rarely invaded. When he came up to the house, his accent receded, his deference came to the fore, and Patricia could hate him. Here...

"I'm all right," she croaked.

"No y'aren't," he said. He wasn't touching her but she could feel the heat coming off him. He smelled of the diesel of the horsetrucks, and of course of the horses. Patricia might have taken a deep breath. She wanted to bury her face in his sweater.

"But you will be," he added.

She'd be a lot better if she could share all the problems of taking over the estate with someone. And the way Daniel was looking at her now, she almost opened her mouth to tell him so. But before she could, he said, "What did you come down here for?"

She couldn't remember. She didn't want to remember. "Umm... the horses."

A dimple appeared in Daniel's cheek. "I thought so."

"Well, yes." She took another breath. She had to get this back on track. Be professional. This man was in charge of several million pounds-worth of the estate's value. Swooning and sighing would not get the job done. "I just... wanted you, when you have a moment, to put together a list of the horses you think we can sell."

As she'd known he would, Daniel's expression shut down at the word, at the idea. "Sell," he said.

"Yes." Though he hadn't moved, a gulf had opened up between them, and the ice coming off him helped her to steel her own spine. "You know the debt we have to pay off. And I only have six months to start paying. We might need that much time to find good buyers for the horses."

The dimple had gone. Sadly. "These horses are all part of the bloodline Gerald and his father worked on for decades."

"Yes, I'm aware of that." Some acerbity crept into her voice. So much for Daniel being the clearheaded one. "And I know as their trainer, each of them is special to you. But—"

"I'm not saying this because they're 'special' to me," he interrupted. "I'm saying this because if you break up the string it will devalue each horse."

"I know it's not ideal, Daniel, but there's no getting around the fact that we must make up the tax bill and the horses are the most valuable assets we own."

"It will devalue the Danby name," he said.

Patricia reared. He'd scored a direct hit and he knew it. Fighting hurt that he could accuse her of throwing away her father's legacy, she steadied herself with one hand on his desk. "The Danby name will be just fine," she said coldly.

His eyes were coal-black sparks of challenge, now. "The Danby string keeps it that way. Break them up and the bloodline will be gone in two generations."

"Then what do you suggest? I must raise this money."

"Sell some land."

If she'd had pearls at her throat, she would have clutched them. As it was, she couldn't stop her hand from covering the pain in her stomach his words had invoked. Yes, the horses were important, but the land was... was *hers*.

"We wouldn't make enough," she said.

"You might. Have you looked into it?"

Of course she hadn't. Some questions you just wanted answered another way.

"Danby's growing. The faster trains from Hawes and the views have made it more desirable, and there aren't enough houses to go around."

Unequal to his logic, her stomachache worsened. "Where?" she asked, breathless.

"I think you know where," he said.

Just like that, their history invaded the conversation and held her spellbound. Daniel's mouth had tightened at the memory and Patricia's heart was in her throat. This was the closest they'd got to mentioning that night in eight years.

Birch Field. Fifty acres of tussocky grassland, almost cut off from the rest of the estate by a stream and a road. Ignored by anyone who worked there, unless you happened to own it. Unless you were about to leave for university and the groom you'd been in love with for ten years had finally given you that look, and you'd both ridden off there and hidden in the folds of the hill and you'd given him everything and then three months later he'd looked through you like nothing had happened. Unless that.

Recalling his face that Christmas helped her to say, "I'm surprised you remember that."

He searched her face for a long time before he answered. She had no idea what she was showing him, but she lifted her chin and raised one eyebrow under his scrutiny. She could show indifference, just as he had.

"It's back there," he said.

Did he mean, back in the distant past, or so insignificant that he couldn't be bothered to call it to mind? "It certainly is," she said anyway.

He frowned. "Tricia, I—"

"I'll make enquiries," she interrupted, goaded by his saying her name that way. He didn't get to be indifferent in one sentence and caring in the next. Her heart couldn't take it. She reminded herself of Hamid's advice about marrying. What would she do with a caring Daniel anyway? If she was going to leave the estate one day, it was better to keep the past in the past, just as Daniel wanted.

Now it was time to step away from him. She forced her feet to move, this time, and as she did so, the sounds of the stable beyond the door behind her seeped into her consciousness. A horse being led beyond the window snickered and a groom's low call clashed with the metallic clang of the horsebox being closed.

"All right," Daniel said. "Look, Trish, I'm not trying to—"

"Yes, thank you, Daniel." She adjusted her scarf at her throat before opening the door, letting the outside in. Blowing away the atmosphere that could never be resolved. "I'll let you know."

She thought he might have come to the door and watched her walk through the yard, watched her nod to the grooms and pause to give a horsenut from the capacious pockets of Gerald's coat to Gazillion. When someone behind her said, "Sir?" he certainly answered quickly and clearly enough. Patricia congratulated herself on not turning back, but walked up the hill to the house, Gazillion's soft muzzle still leaving a sensation on her palm.

5

And so, loath as she was to do it, Patricia looked up land values, school enrollments, and train times. It wasn't just the memory of that particular part of the estate that made her reluctant to call an estate agent. Her great-grandfather had jumped through so many hoops to keep the land intact, after the First World War had changed the lifestyles of the landed gentry for ever. The horses had been part of that, and now they were not enough. She felt that she was letting down the side if she could keep neither the horses nor the land together.

The numbers involved did surprise her. She wouldn't even have to sell the entire plot to get the money she needed. As soon as she started googling the subject, ads from developers began popping up in sidebars, begging for land to build on. She also couldn't miss all the news stories about the housing shortage across the country. As though even the BBC was against her.

Fine, she admitted to herself a few days later, as she waited for a visit from Sophia and Hannah and her stomach rumbled from waiting for her tea. *People need houses. I've had my head in the sand. Elitist, out-of-touch aristo. Everything Daniel's expression has been telling me for eight years.*

At least Sophia and Hannah would be on her side. At least they'd understand. They walked in with the same flurry and fanfare as a landing helicopter, and were soon several sandwiches and cups of tea in.

Her friends had kept up a steady conversation of gossip and trifles, but now Hannah put out a hand to grip Patricia's (just as she was about to reach for a fourth homemade Jaffa cake). "So how are things going?" she said. "Did James really leave you in the lurch?"

"Not in the lurch," Patricia countered. "He was never going to stay. I knew that. He knows nothing about taking care of the estate, and I do."

"Too much," Sophia put in. "Gerald relied on you too much."

Patricia couldn't take criticism of Gerald. "Not strictly true, darling. He left me alone much of the time after uni."

"He didn't need after uni. You learned it all before we finished Harrington."

"And I'm glad about it. What if he'd waited? What if I didn't know anything and then he'd..."

Hannah squeezed her hand tighter. "We're sorry, darling. Sophia didn't mean to malign your father. Did you, Soph?"

"Of course not. Sorry. Have a Jaffa cake."

Patricia nibbled the chocolate and orange off one side of the biscuit. Cake. Whatever it was. "Anyway. There *are* still plenty of things I didn't learn."

"What?" asked Hannah. "Is it the horses? Maybe Padraig could help you?"

"She doesn't need Padraig for the horses, silly," Sophia chided her. "She has Daniel."

"Ah." Hannah tipped her head to look at Patricia, who was now turning the Jaffa cake in a circle in her fingers, looking with studious intent for the next side to attack. Determined not to let her face change. "So we're here already. How is Daniel?"

Patricia took a bite and pointed to her mouth to show how it was simply impossible for her to answer just then.

"That's all right," Hannah said knowingly. "We'll wait."

Patricia rolled her eyes and swallowed. "Fine." Though she still took a sip of tea before she went on. "We've only seen each other once since the funeral, and he wasted no time in reminding me how elitist and out of touch I am."

Her friends reacted with gratifying shock and hurt. "Darling," Sophia protested. "You with your charity? And what was your degree in again?"

"Social anthropology."

At university she'd travelled widely and studied all kinds of different cultures. Had it all become just a theory to her? Had she really forgotten about the people who relied on her father and the estate? Not even them, because tenants and employees were a part of her job.

"He wants me to sell some land on the south edge of the property, near the village. He says I could get all the money I need from it."

"How does that make you elitist?"

"Because I didn't think of it first." She looked at them in supplication. "I didn't even think that someone else could use any of our land better than I can. That I can actually fulfil a need by selling the land. That people are crying out for property and I sit here in twenty-four bedrooms and a thousand acres and—"

"Trish, sweetie," Sophia interrupted, while Hannah held her hand in a deathgrip. "We've all been through the guilt-mill. Every time I see the statistics on the price of new homes, I've half a mind to call Rutledge and hand over my fields."

"We can argue the class structure and *noblesse oblige* and all that until the cows come home," added Hannah, "but the truth is that every decision you make about this estate is for the good of everyone on it. And when people come to the open days in the main house, do they not go and spend their money in the village as well?"

"Yes, but. I still should have listened sooner."

"Well, now, if we're going to get on the subject of listening to Daniel, that's a very different kettle of fish."

"Just out of interest," Sophia said as Patricia blushed, "how were you going to raise the money?"

"Selling the horses." Their expressions reflected their dislike of that idea. "Well, the horses are our most portable asset!" she defended herself. "I didn't mean all of them. Just maybe some of the foals and one of the stallions."

"Which one?" Sophia asked. "Which one could you live without?"

"Which one could Daniel live without, you mean," Hannah interjected.

Patricia threw up her hands, dislodging Hannah's grip. "He already told me what a bad idea it is. I still think some of them could go, and I still think keeping as much land as possible in the estate is good for farming, and for our future tax burden. I have to look into it more, but..." She sighed, deflating. "He was right. And I hate that."

She was looking at her teacup but could feel Sophia and Hannah exchange looks above her. "Why is that so terrible?" asked Sophia.

Patricia flapped her hands in front of her. "The whole thing is wrong," she said desperately. "Daniel coming here in the first place, when I was too young to... to put up barricades against him. His position, then and now. And I don't mean his class," she added hurriedly. "I mean, he's an employee. I write his cheques. If either of us does something wrong, he might leave and then where would the stables be? And if we lose the stables, we lose the life of this place."

"She does mean his class," Sophia pointed out to Hannah over Patricia's head. "If he was one of James' friends from uni, we wouldn't be having this conversation even if she did sign his cheques."

"That's not fair," Patricia tried. "*He's* the one who makes it about class. All that 'my lady'-ing and virtual forelock tugging and whatnot. Anything to keep me—" Her hands were fascinating again.

"And how close have *you* tried to get to *him*?" asked Hannah. "Did *you* try to cross the divide?"

"All the time," she insisted. But not since that night. Not since the following Christmas.

That walking cliché Bernard Smythe-Thomas had come home with her. His father owned half of Derbyshire and they'd grown up in the same circles, but she'd almost never spoken to him until they'd ended up at St. Andrew's together. Bernard told her he wanted to meet James and talk with them both about projects like the one that eventually drew James out of the country. During the holidays, Gerald wanted anyone and everyone to come and stay to distract him from the loss of his wife, Patricia and James' mother. Patricia couldn't think of a good enough reason not to invite Bernard and so he'd come.

And begun a revolting campaign to get her into one of the guest bedrooms. Or the yellow sitting room. Or the corridor between the armor room and the servants' stairs. He wasn't violent but he was persistent, and Patricia's innate politeness couldn't find the right words to make him understand he was being rejected. Pretty soon the servants were looking at them as a couple, and she had to stop Sarah mid-sentence when the woman asked, with appropriate diffidence, if she'd like to move Bernard's room closer to hers.

By Christmas Eve she'd had barely a moment to rest, unless she was in her room. Her responsibilities as hostess meant that she hadn't had time to go to the stables, even if she hadn't felt a shyness about seeing Daniel again. Sophia was also staying with her and she'd just plucked up the courage to invite her out for a ride, where she would tell her that she was going to throw Bernard out and might need backup, when Gerald issued his usual invitation to all the employees to join them for carols in the Great Hall.

The oldest part of the house, the Hall was Tudor and featured a fireplace the size of Gerald's horse, and paneling from trees five hundred years old when Henry VIII had been a boy. It was usually freezing, but DaShawn's predecessor had hauled in enough logs for a siege and in any case, the mead (all right, hot buttered rum, but the effect was the same) was flowing. The crowd pressed together, guests and employees elbow to elbow, all singing lustily while Gerald's bass thundered along beneath them.

Patricia couldn't help but look out for Daniel among the faces, but she was near the front and the grooms and yard-hands had come in last. Also, not to put too fine a point on it, Daniel was too tall for a jockey but he wasn't all that tall, and while she thought perhaps she'd caught sight of his dark rumpled hair, she couldn't be sure.

Bernard, unfortunately, found her. "Tight squeeze, what?" he shouted, putting his face too close to hers, his arm stealing around her waist. Patricia tried to twist away without revealing her dilemma to the person next to her, but only succeeded in turning a circle so that Bernard's hand could stay exactly where it was. She put up her own hand to push his off, but elbowed a neighbor and had to spend her time apologizing.

Bernard put his mouth to her ear as Gerald began a rumbling rendition of *Good King Wenceslas*. "I know we're all terribly egalitarian and all that, but couldn't your father at least have kept the stablehands out until later? The heat's terrible and I'm sure I can smell the horseshit from here."

Brightly shone the moon that night
Though the frost was cruel

Patricia shuddered and opened her mouth to answer but the singing was so loud she lost her chance, and in that hesitation, Bernard took the last few inches and kissed her ear.

Politeness be damned. She snapped her head back and gave him her best death-stare, the one she saved for egregious breaches of conduct among the servants. He leered back. So she pushed away from him, not caring what direction she went in as long as it was away.

She'd been shuffling closer to the back than she'd thought. The gardeners and groomsmen surrounded her, and when they squeezed back to let her through, she saw Daniel, not two people away. He couldn't have heard what Bernard had said, or seen what he'd done, but the look he gave her was as cool as though he didn't recognize her any more. For their first exchange of looks since that night in the field, this wasn't the expression she was expecting.

The next time she'd been able to get any time alone with him, after Bernard had been packed off and she'd finally had a chance to come to the stables, she'd said, "Did you hear what Bernard said?"

He'd straightened up from brushing one of the mares. "Who, my lady?"

And that was when he'd started calling her "my lady."

"Bernard Smythe—never mind. The man who was standing with me at the carol singing last week."

This was not the conversation she'd wanted to have. She'd wanted to stare at his mouth and remember the smell of the crushed grass, the slightly metallic sound of the stream at their feet. She wanted him to look as though he wanted to pull her into his arms, though they both knew he couldn't, with the open top to the stable door and the people walking past outside. She wanted him to say, as he had afterwards back in September, "Are y'all right, lass?" and she could have answered, "I've never been better," and he could have at least looked as though he wanted to kiss her hairline and settle her more firmly into his arms.

But none of that happened. And it could only be because he'd heard what Bernard said. Or seen him kiss her. "Bernard's not my boyfriend," she blurted out, which was a stupid thing to say, and not what she'd wanted at all.

"No, my lady," he said, his tone as indifferent as though he'd started his job last week.

"He's a... listen, Daniel, could you stop saying 'my lady' like that?"

Some ice crept into his voice. "Just remembering my place."

Pain bloomed in her chest. "Why are you saying that? You *did* hear what he said!"

"I heard... enough. To remind me."

"That's not fair." God, if she could just touch him. But she couldn't. There was no privacy in the stables. Daniel slept in a dorm with five other men. "Do you think I'm like him?"

"I think you... will have to be."

She was eighteen years old, and in that moment her pain was replaced with anger as fast as love could become hate. "I think *you're* the snob," she spat, in a low voice so it wouldn't carry outside. "A reverse snob. Believing as little of me as

Bernard did of you is just as classist as what you think I've done." She looked at him, at the coating of dust from Rabadan's grooming. At his flat cap, which she'd always found so charming before but now saw as a symbol of his desire to keep himself separate from her. "With an attitude like that, then yes, I'll never be able to understand you."

His jaw was tight. "I suppose that means you were roughing it, then, back in September," he said. "Just another primitive culture to study, was I?"

Patricia reeled. That he could dismiss that night... That he could think so little of her... That he could even say those words, knowing her as long as he had. Heat began behind her eyes, but she was never going to let him see her vulnerable again. "And I was just another slag you could brag to your football hooligan friends about," she hissed. "Is that right?"

Now his head snapped back. "Don't say that—"

"Oh, *now* you're going to be circumspect?" Shaking with rage and hurt and knowing she would cry if she didn't leave, she wrestled the bolt on the half-door until it shot back with a sat-isfying clang that made Rabadan shy. He hated loud noises, and Daniel had his hands full sooth-ing him, so Patricia had time to flee.

She'd never been alone with him again, until Gerald had left them in the ladies' loo at Ascot.

"All right, no. I haven't tried. And neither has he." Patricia poured more tea and gave Hannah the milk jug. "We both know we couldn't make anything of it, even if I wanted to."

Hannah snorted. "'Even if you wanted to.' Tr-ish, darling, I've never seen someone want some-thing more. Who are you kidding?"

Patricia shook her head. "No one. Hamid even pointed it out."

Now Hannah's shock was comical. "Hamid warned you off Daniel?"

"No, not in so many words. Oh, I've had enough tea. Who wants a G&T?"

Neither of her guests was going to say no to that, even if it was barely four o'clock. Patricia pressed the bell and soon they were clinking glasses filled with Hendricks, ice and thinly-sliced cucumber. *Elitist indeed. Well, I yam what I yam*, as she'd heard them say when she'd been in New York.

The distraction had also moved the conversation away from Hamid, but then, as if summoned by the mention of his name, DaShawn was announcing him.

6

Never one for appointments, Hamid had often paid impromptu visits when Gerald had been alive, and Patricia had no reason to suppose he'd remember to ask now. Still, she could have done without his arrival just when she and two friends were snouts-down in gin in the middle of the afternoon.

"Hello, Hamid," she said, walking over to greet him as he entered the drawing room behind DaShawn.

"Hello, my dear," Hamid said. Patricia lifted her cheek for a kiss. She hoped she smelled like cucumber and not alcohol.

"You remember my friends?" She rattled off Sophia and Hannah's full names and titles (Sophia's being the more impressive—Hannah had lost hers when she'd married Padraig).

"Yes, indeed." Hamid's tall, slightly-greying-but-still-handsome looks were not lost on either girl, nor his opinion about alcohol, but they offered their hands and looked as pleased to see him as if he were a member of their own families.

"I am interrupting," he said. But before anyone could say, "Not at all," or "That's quite all right," or even offer him a sandwich, he went on. "I have just returned from my trip, Patricia, and there is something particular I would like to discuss with you. And Daniel. If you don't mind, I've asked him to come up here so I can speak to you both together."

A pause of a few seconds passed before Patricia could stammer out the required response. Sophia and Hannah had taken their seats again and now sat huddled together on the couch. Patricia could bet they were hoping she'd forget they were there, so they could hear whatever it was Hamid wanted to say.

"Would you like to meet him in my father's study?" she asked, because she knew why Hamid was there and Daniel would not appreciate a discussion of his career in front of her friends.

"Whatever you prefer, my dear."

"After you," she said, and when he'd preceded her out of the door she looked back at the others. Sophia's lower lip was wobbling on purpose, and Hannah's hands were clasped together in front of her in a silent plea. "Stay there," Patricia whispered. "Don't get drunk. I'll be back when I can."

They sighed and she heard them clink glasses as she closed the door.

One day she would stop calling this room Gerald's study, but at the moment it screamed his name as loudly as it had on the day of his funeral. Hamid waited for her to open the door for him, which she appreciated as it showed respect for her as the head of the house—unlike his unexpected arrival, but she couldn't have everything. "Tea?" she asked automatically, though she was waterlogged with the stuff now. He nodded and so she rang the bell again, asking for tea for three. The tray arrived at the same time as Daniel, who wore a blazer and trousers far too tidy to have been worn in the stable.

Hamid stood to shake his hand, even though he must have seen him not fifteen minutes before, and said, "Excellent, Daniel. I am so glad that you are home today." Forgetting himself for a minute, he indicated that Daniel sit.

Daniel glanced at Patricia. They hadn't met since their conversation about the land. She hadn't even gone riding unless she knew he was away at a race. Perhaps he was being polite, or perhaps he was, again, rubbing her nose in their difference in station. "Oh, do sit down," she said; it was a hairsbreadth away from being a snap.

Hamid was at the large round table that stood in the bay window, so they all sat there, and he began to pull papers from a briefcase. Patricia was reminded for a moment of the reading of Gerald's will, and her lips tightened. She had a feeling that this interview was going to shake up her life just as much as that one had.

"Well, Daniel," Hamid began, "I've been in the States for the last week or so. Can you guess why?"

Daniel's eyebrows went up. "No, sir."

"I'm starting a string out there. A new bloodline. Patricia," he said, turning to her with a big smile, "can you guess whose?"

Daniel's face looked as frozen as Patricia's felt. Her voice came out as a whisper. "Gerald's?"

"That's right." He held out his hands, his golden pinky ring glittering in the light coming through the long windows. "I can solve your tax problem, my dear. And it will only cost you your trainer."

Daniel took in a breath so quick it made him cough. "What?"

"It's all right, Daniel," Hamid assured him. "Gerald knew that I would ask you. I'm offering you an opportunity to grow that the English racing season simply cannot give you. We can take the Danby horses and create a bloodstock that will stand in America for generations."

Daniel just stared at him. Patricia said, "When you say, 'take the Danby horses'…"

"I will buy the entire stable from you, my dear." While she was still gaping at the numbers that flew into her head at that sentence, he added, "Bar one or two whom I'm sure you will want for your own use. I'll also take whichever of your staff would like to come. It will be a state of the art facility in Bedminster, New Jersey. It is out in the country but only thirty minutes to Newark Airport: they can come and visit whenever they wish."

"But I... But I..." Daniel was saying. His brain must have been malfunctioning as badly as hers. She'd known Hamid would poach him, but not for this. Not to be thousands of miles away. Not to take Gerald's life's work with him.

Hamid was still smiling as though he were giving them both a great gift. "Do you not see, my dear, that without the stable, you will have fewer cares? You can go on and find that husband we were talking about—"

She blushed as red as Hamid's ruby tie-pin. "We didn't—" She would *not* look at Daniel.

Hamid waved a hand. "I think you agreed with my principle. Perhaps James will come back without the worry of a stable to take care of as well as everything else."

But Daniel took care of the stable, she thought dumbly. *He took care of all of it.*

"Your offer is very generous, sir," Daniel finally said. "But I've lived here my whole life. I don't know if I could—"

"All the more reason that you should broaden your horizons, my boy. How old are you now? Thirty?"

Yes, he's thirty. So not a boy. But she had to bridle in silence.

"Yes."

"Did you plan on staying here for ever? With your talents? Forgive me, Patricia," he nodded to her, "but Daniel, you are wasted here. In the States you can stretch your formidable mind. You could be a household name."

That was overstating it rather. Trainers didn't get to be on the lips of people outside the racing world. Horses, yes. Not owners or trainers. Perhaps Hamid was hoping to change that.

"Oh, and I didn't tell you the best part. Your starting salary would be—" and he named a figure that was more than their best stallion's last stud fee.

If Daniel worked for her for the rest of his life, Patricia would never be able to match that salary. And she'd bet it came with a big American house, not the sweet but shabby cottage that Daniel had lived in for two years.

"That... that's very generous," said Daniel, while Patricia's heart curled into itself. "I appreciate your faith in me."

She looked at him as though he was leaving with Hamid today, as though she'd never see him again. At his navy blazer and dark trousers, which Gerald might have helped him buy so he would blend in with the rest of the horse world. Despite his careful grooming, his smart shoes held a trace of dust on them from the stable. His cap and the green padded jacket he always wore must have been put away by DaShawn when he'd come into the house.

His face was as familiar to her as her own. The high cheekbones and sharp jaw of a man who ate sparingly; the dark, deepset eyes that had looked at her with tolerance and affection, and one night, with desire and, she'd hoped, love. His brown hair, stick-straight apart from the cowlick which even now was beginning to make itself known. His skin, pale in winter, tan in summer, indifferent to heat and cold if it meant his horses were taken care of first.

Without the horses, Danby would become something else. Without Daniel, Patricia wasn't sure if she cared to find what that was.

Yet, if he wanted to go with Hamid, how could she stop him? Ask him to refuse a career and a lifestyle that Daniel's family, in their council flat in Middlesbrough, could hardly have dreamed of? It was common knowledge that he still gave much of his salary to his mother.

"I'd like to think about it," he said, which allowed Patricia to take a breath. He wasn't going today. She had time to school her response.

"Certainly," said Hamid, though he looked less than thrilled at their quiet reactions.

"Can I let you know next week? By this time next week. I'll let you know one way or the other."

"Yes, my boy, but I do hope you are seeing the opportunity. Here." Hamid pushed the papers he'd taken out of his briefcase across the table. "Here's the prospectus for the land, and some examples of stables in the area. The U.S. Equestrian Team practice there." His gaze drifted off for a moment. Patricia was sure he was imagining the glory of breeding a horse that might be used in the Olympics.

"Thank you, sir. I'll look it over carefully." Daniel gathered the papers into a neat rectangle, then stuck out his hand across the table to shake Hamid's. "Thank you," he said again. How could he not? What had Patricia done for him lately?

"Certainly, certainly," Hamid smiled, taking Daniel's hand in two of his, forcing them both to stretch a little over the table. "And Patricia? The horses?"

Oh, God. She was going to have to make that decision, as well. She unstuck her tongue from the roof of her mouth. "Would you give me a week, too, Hamid?"

He let go of Daniel and wagged a finger at her. "You are always so measured, Patricia. Would you not jump at the chance to pay your bills all in one fell swoop?"

Her smile was thin. "As you say: measured response. I will let you know as soon as I can, and at the latest, by next Thursday."

Hamid conceded and pushed his chair back, rubbing his thighs. "Well, then, I've said everything I came to say. Is there anything you need from me, my dear? Any other way I can help you in this difficult transition?"

"You're very kind," Patricia said, standing and telling her knees to stop shaking. "So far, so normal. No news is good news."

She walked him to the front door with Daniel and they shook hands again there. But when Hamid left, Daniel did not follow him, but stood motionless, his eyes black on hers.

"Congratulations," she made herself say. "What an opportunity—"

But he held up a hand. "Trish. Don't say a word." His jaw was rigid. She could almost feel his teeth grinding.

"All right. Gracious, you act as though it were my idea."

"To sell all the horses? Isn't that what you wanted?"

"*No!* I told you already, just a few. Perhaps we could syndicate Gazillion or Roundtree." Roundtree Chanticleer was their Grand National-winning stallion, now pulling in stud fees as fast as he could get his breath back.

"What," he said, as if he hadn't heard her, "about a husband?"

The change in topic almost snapped her neck back. "That's just Hamid... looking out for me."

"He's finding you a husband?" Now he barely moved his lips.

"Not..." She hesitated, though she didn't know why. Was some small, eighteen-year-old part of herself hoping to make him jealous? What good would that do? "No, of course not," she said more firmly.

Over Daniel's shoulder, she noticed that Sophia and Hannah had crept out of the drawing room and were hugging the door, listening. Daniel saw her head lift and followed her gaze.

"Hello, Daniel!" called Sophia.

"Viscountess," Daniel nodded to her. "Mrs. MacDermott," he added to Hannah.

"Are you off-duty now?" Sophia went on. "It's past five o'clock. Will you join us in a G&T?"

Patricia threw her daggers but Daniel said, "No, thank you. I need to get back for evening stables."

DaShawn had appeared out of nowhere with Daniel's hat and coat. Patricia watched Daniel's every move, while her skin itched to touch him and her heart ached that she couldn't.

"My lady," he said.

"Daniel," she replied faintly, more of a plea than a farewell. But he—damn him—touched the peak of his hat and walked out of the door DaShawn held open.

Sophia and Hannah swooped on her like bats in pastel summer dresses. "What did he say? Why did he leave so fast? What did Hamid want with both of you?"

"Make me a fresh G&T first," Patricia said grimly. "And this time, just wave the tonic bottle over the glass."

7

Patricia couldn't sleep. She felt as though each of her horses in turn was galloping through her head. Not nearly as soothing as sheep. At two o'clock in the morning she gave up, got up, and wrapped Gerald's dressing gown around her. It was made of a quilted material almost as thick as a rug, and the warm July night was really too much for it, but Patricia needed his scent around her tonight.

Not bothering with slippers, she padded through the empty house. Past the fourteen guest bedrooms and James', which held all his university paraphernalia and not much else, through the green reading room where her great-grandmother, the Princess, and her siblings had played cat's cradle on rainy days when they were too old for the nursery. Patricia's shadow was cast across the portraits hanging on the wall of the south gallery by the full moon illuminating the windows. She glanced outside and saw a fox scamper across the lawn. Good hunting night, though the fox was just as visible as its prey.

She took hold of the railing that her mother had touched when she came down the stairs to marry Gerald, when he was a young man with a crazy 'Seventies moustache and sideburns, and a uniform that had been designed in the nineteenth century. The old wood always felt a little warm to her fingers; it was so wide her hand would not go around it. James had slid down it once and fallen off, breaking his leg on the black and white marble floor below, which was the only thing that had stopped Gerald from giving him a hiding. *Not the fault of the banister*, she thought as always, giving it a little pat as she stepped off the red-carpeted staircase.

The white portions of the front hall floor were luminous in the light the moon was sending in from every window, and Patricia could see her way to Gerald's study easily. She turned the ancient brass handle and the heavy door opened.

Gerald's smell was fading. The realization brought a lump to her throat, so she went around the table where she, Hamid and Daniel had sat this afternoon, to the faded velvet curtains, where she gathered their heavy folds up to her face and breathed in.

There he was: Ardbeg and cigars and saddle soap and grass after rain, and Patricia cried into the fabric until she had no tears left.

When she'd found some tissues in the water closet hidden behind a bookcase, Patricia stayed by the window, leaning on the open curtains, looking out at the moon-filled night. She thought she could see the light left on in the stables at the foot of the hill; it flickered yellow in the moon's blue gaze. The stables themselves were dark humps against the deep green of the hills behind them. The difference in light made them seem almost like sleeping creatures, hunkered down out of the wind.

If Patricia were to go to the other end of this window, she would see the Victorian-era fountain that sat in the center of the pea-graveled driveway. They only turned it on now when they were open to the public, as the water use in the height of summer was prohibitive. So she would only have seen the stone dolphins balancing a ball in the style of the Sovereign's Orb, its cross restored by Gerald's father after a century and a half of erosion. One of her favourite sights as a child had been to see the family carriage, led by four matching black horses, do two circuits of the drive before stopping at the portico to take Gerald to whatever formal event he was bound for. Her mother was mixed up in those memories, though she'd died when Patricia was small and her reality was as vague as the authenticity of those dolphins.

Now that Gerald was gone and James would not be here to attend those functions, should Patricia sell the carriage? Who on earth would buy it? Hamid? Some other oil billionaire? Someone from Texas? She shuddered, swaying the fabric at the window.

Still, America was where Daniel's future might be. And though he'd made fun of the Americans just as much as she did—as they all did, for heaven's sake, all the while aware that it was American money that had just about saved the

British aristocracy—he might within a few months be breathing their air, living on their land, digging up their fields for Gerald's—for *her*—horses.

She probed her feelings about the horses. Thought about how she'd felt when Niger and Noir, two of the black beauties who had pulled the carriage, had died of old age. Kala and Nero were living out their final days in the lower field. She'd hired horses to pull the carriage at Gerald's funeral. When Breath of Air's foal had staked itself and had to be put down, she'd cried and even Daniel's eyes had been wet. But that was the summer after their estrangement, and she'd held herself off from offering him sympathy.

Patricia threw herself into the capacious chair at Gerald's leather desk and tucked her knees under her chin. How many times had she actually seen Daniel since that night? Actually seen him? Let alone talked to him? Tried to talk to him? She thought of coming home from uni: three times a year, plus a few weekends. She'd summered in Nice, Barcelona, Monaco. Flirted with Andrea Casiraghi, the grandson of Grace Kelly. Wintered in Glasgow, working with at-risk teens, raising awareness for the charity which had eventually asked her to be their patron. When she'd gone home she'd ridden on the land, but she'd often been with friends, so even if Daniel had brought out her horse, she couldn't have done more than smile at him. And she'd been young, and hurt, so she hadn't. In any case, Daniel was soon assistant trainer and had people under him to hand her the reins of her favourite piebald, Romany, and toss her into the saddle.

So, all told, ten times in three years? And maybe three of those times that she could have talked to him? He'd certainly never come as close to her again after the Christmas carol singing. After university she'd begun dividing her time between learning the estate business from Gerald and her charity. Now that she was buried in the estate, she was grateful to Gerald for freeing up some money for her to send to the charity. Such a sum could begin the building of a new shelter, but she would have to carve out a few days soon to check up on it and the charges she took responsibility for.

There had been men, and there had been no reason not to bring them home, especially if they loved horses, or hunting. Or if they were from a different country and knew nothing about York-shire. She'd holidayed in New York, Brisbane, Kuala Lumpur. At home she lived and worked in the house, and while she and Daniel might meet in the halls as he came to speak to Gerald, he'd only ever called her "my lady" and his eyes had hardened and she'd hated him for it. So she'd turned up her nose and looked at her Cartier watch and got in a shot of her own, and then she'd spend the next few days avoiding him.

When Gerald appointed Daniel to head trainer, he'd made it clear that he wanted her at the meetings. "Hislop was on the way out, old girl. No need for you to listen to his old chuffing," he'd said. "But I want you and Daniel to be able to work together. I want you to hear his ideas. They're good ones."

"How will I know that?" she'd protested. "You know about the stock and the bloodlines and all that."

"I know I do. I have it all written down." He'd pointed to the notebooks behind him on the bookcase. "My point is that Daniel does as well, as much as I do and sometimes more. He's birthed some of these foals himself, you know."

She did know. Before that night, she'd once assisted at a birth. She'd been fifteen, then, and already in love with him for over five years. Not love. Was it love when your entire being could have no thought but to catch the next glimpse of him riding out with the string, or brushing down a sweaty horse, his own back soaked, his boots muddy, but not caring until his charge was seen to?

In the years before university there had been no hiding up at the house until she was sure he'd gone to a race. She'd been at the stables almost every day she was home from boarding school. Gerald made her and James learn to muck out the stables, saddle the horses, take care of the tack. James was missing the tip of one finger where a friendly but near-sighted old mare had taken too big a bite of a carrot. Gerald had talked to them about the racing, the comportment of the bloodline, what he looked for, but most of it went over Patricia's head, since she was looking at Daniel's comportment, Daniel's thighs as he posted a trot on Authentic, their broadest stallion at the time; Daniel's face under his racing helmet, a drop of sweat tempting her at his jaw. Patricia had always been grateful to the fencing around the school arena, for holding her up while she observed this.

Lust had come long after love, if not even beginning to imagine her life without him in it was love. One day he'd been her conscientious teacher, showing her the easiest way to fork hay into the feeders, the next she'd been all arms and legs around him, feeling stupid and ugly and wishing she'd never been born because she no longer knew what do to with herself. Yet Gerald had noticed her nascent attempts to avoid the stables and had driven her down there himself if she wouldn't go alone. She'd woken up early once to put on makeup and blow-dry her hair before going down. Most unfortunately, Gerald had already been at morning gallops and had given her one hard look and a nod of his chin that could have dislocated his neck, and Patricia had slunk back to the house to wash her face and put her hair back. When she'd returned, Daniel had smiled at her, and suddenly all her limbs were in exactly the right place.

Her final summer before uni had been one long campaign to get Daniel to notice her again, to change the spark in his eyes when he saw her. There was the inconvenience of an internship at a charity run by her aunt which took her to London for a month, and there was Gerald, but she came down to morning gallops one morning when the dew was still on the grass, and Daniel looked down from Authentic and she looked up and smiled at him, and his eyes blazed and she was altogether lost.

"Tricia," he said the first time she followed him into a stall and watched him clip Romany's tail hairs. "You don't come around any more."

Everyone else called her Trish, including Gerald. One extra syllable and the stall became theirs. Hers and his alone.

"I'm here now," she said.

"I can see that," he said, his mouth turning up on one side.

He didn't speak again but they didn't need to. Their silences said as much as the few words they were able to say when they were alone.

"Do you know where you're going with this?" he asked one time.

"Absolutely," she said, looking him right in the eye. She was going to lose her virginity before she went to college, and she was going to brand herself on Daniel's memory so that he couldn't possibly forget about her while she was away.

He'd put down the feed buckets he'd been holding and held her challenge with a look of his own. "If I were one of your Hooray Henrys," he said, his voice low, "would I be a gentleman about this?"

"If you were one of my Hooray Henrys," she murmured back, "I wouldn't want you like this."

He'd breathed out, then, a shaking sigh of anticipation that sustained Patricia for two weeks, until Gerald went to a race and Daniel stayed home. "Saddle Romany," she said after evening stables one night when everyone else had gone to the pub.

"You saddle her," he'd smiled.

♦

Patricia's feet were cold. She tucked Gerald's dressing gown around them and focused on the desk in front of her. Her laptop was on it now, with two monitors and a separate keyboard to save her from carpal tunnel. Daniel's updated technology had included a breeding software program, and she was going to be transferring Gerald's notes into it as soon as things quieted down.

In the quiet hum of the backup drive under the desk, Patricia finished counting how many times she'd seen Daniel since that night. Not enough, but too many not to blame herself for keeping him at arm's length for so long. He was older than she, it was true, and so could have been the grown-up about the misunderstanding. But Patricia had held all the power to change their dynamic and she'd chosen not to. Feudalism aside, she was Daniel's boss, as near as dammit, and should have either committed to that or tossed it aside and told him how she really felt.

Of course it was only now that he was leaving that she would admit what she'd known all along: that love was indeed an inadequate word for what he meant to her. She might even call it a business-like longing, since under his care the stable was thriving and Gerald's name would be respected for years to come.

If the string stayed.

Even if Daniel took it to America, Danby would still be a name to be reckoned with, on a larger stage with more races, more chances to win.

Daniel would thrive, too. He might take his mother to Vegas, or his nephews and nieces to Disneyland, or... well, she didn't know what was in New Jersey. A shore?

Or he could stay in Yorkshire. She could ask him to keep the string here, work for her as always. She could try and pay him more. She could sell that piece of land and use it to pay the taxes so she could keep the string. And Daniel.

She could at least show him that she respected his advice.

She reached forward and picked up the heavy old-fashioned phone on Gerald's desk. Under it were four clunky buttons. Three went to the kitchens, Gerald's part-time secretary, and Patricia's cell. One went to Daniel's office at the stables.

But a ringing phone with only a window between the office and the yard might disturb the horses, or wake the lads who had to be up in two hours. Patricia glanced at the window. She could see the merest rim of lighter indigo dusting the treeline on the far hills. Dawn came early to Yorkshire in the summer, and the horses got restless and needed exercise. Patricia put her chin on her tucked-up knee. She had no idea of the sacrifices Daniel had made to work for Gerald.

She put the phone down again, the sudden cutoff of the dialtone making the silence seem louder. *In three hours*, she promised herself.

8

She was exhausted from sitting up, thinking about Daniel and her future, then falling asleep forty-five minutes before she was supposed to call him, on a long formal sofa Gerald had kept in the study for that purpose. She'd woken when Jessica had come looking for her at seven o'clock.

"Aw, lass," Jessica had said with all the sympathy of someone who knew grief when she saw it, and even though she was supposed to call Patricia "my lady," and she was almost Patricia's age, she looked on her employer like an aunt offering comfort to her beloved niece.

"I'm fine," Patricia affirmed, sitting up and stretching. Gerald's dressing gown fell off her. At some point she'd taken it off and draped it over herself instead. The heavy, embroidered fabric was as good as a blanket. "Really."

"I brought your tea," Jessica said, apparently not inclined to believe her. "And Mrs. Gennaro can bring your breakfast in here if you'd like."

"No, that's not—" But she looked at the table by the window. Why not? "Actually, that would be lovely. But no fuss. Just a knife and fork and the plate. Really." DaShawn liked laying tables, and if she didn't stop him he'd have a four-course place setting in front of her by eight o'clock, and she'd never eat.

Jessica carried a tea tray in from the hall and set it on the round table. Patricia liked seeing the delicate china on Gerald's heavy old furnishings. She moved to the window herself and looked back at the room from there. The curtains would go, and perhaps a few of the heavier pieces of furniture. Some of the unused books. And she'd bring in flowers. A riotous burst of white peonies in a blue jug would set off her breakfast perfectly.

"Ah, lass," Jessica said again. "I miss him, too. He were always so polite to us. Nothing were too much trouble if he could help us out." She arranged the milk by Patricia's right hand. "Now you just set there and relax, and DaShawn'll bring you your eggs."

"I'm all right, Jessica," Patricia insisted. "Really." And she was. The night had changed her. No more shrines to Gerald. He wouldn't like it and neither did she. She wasn't finished grieving him: not by a long shot. But the horses were his legacy; she was going to make the rest of the estate hers. And hang James and any little bint he might by some miracle bring home. And hang Hamid, too, while she was at it, though she might shock him with a hug of gratitude for his care of her before she sent him packing.

When Jessica left, Patricia padded back to the desk and this time, put through the call.

"Patricia?" Daniel said.

Not "my lady."

It was a symbol of what she would change that he called her by her name. "Good morning, Daniel," she said pleasantly, easily.

"Is everything all right?"

She laughed. Yes, he would think that, after her tone to him for eight years. "Yes. It's fine." She was going to have to find a new word for fine. "I wondered if you would have time in the next few days to ride with me down to the Birch Field."

He didn't speak for a moment. Patricia bit her lip so she wouldn't launch into explanations. She wanted to say this face-to-face, and without any chance of interruption.

"Of course," he said at last. "If you like."

"Good," she said. "When?"

"I'm leaving for Newcastle tomorrow morning."

Damn. Would she have to hold onto this speech all weekend? "All right," she said resignedly. "So—"

"So it'd better be this afternoon."

Her heart sped up and her bare toes curled into the oriental rug. So soon? "Oh. Oh, well, good. If you can spare the time."

"I can." Could she hear that one-sided smile of his down the phone line?

"Good," she said again. "Thank you."

"What time?"

Yes, right. What time? She was so taken aback that he was making time for her today that she could only stare at the sun slanting through the window for a moment, before her brain kicked in again. "I'll come by at twelve." DaShawn came in at that moment with her breakfast on another silver tray. It gave her an idea. "I'll ask Mrs. Gennaro to make us a packed lunch."

His silence showed that she'd surprised him this time. "Sounds... efficient."

"All right, then. I'll see you at twelve."

DaShawn put the tray on the table in the window. "The visitors, my lady," he said delicately.

She looked down at her nightshirt, which was half off one shoulder and showed more leg than she reckoned DaShawn had expected to see this early in the morning. Bits of her hair were floating in front of her face, probably because she had a tangled nest on one side of her head. And Gerald's dressing gown was still crumpled on the sofa. "Yes, yes. You're right." The Hall opened to the public at nine o'clock. Gerald's office, and a few other rooms as well as most of the first floor, were out of bounds, but still. "I'll get cleaned up."

"Very good, my lady."

"If it's all right with Mrs. Gennaro," she went on, "I'd like to see her when I'm dressed."

"I'll let her know to expect you," DaShawn said in his dour, butler-certified voice.

He had to go, and she had to eat, but Patricia allowed herself to give him a knowing smile. "Catch the game last night, did you?"

"Yes, my lady. Bloody criminal, my lady." And they exchanged grins that crossed the line from employer/employee to colleagues. DaShawn helped her run the house and knew as much about the objects in it as she did. He'd had to leave university in his second year to take care of his dying mother. Gerald had met him on a visit to a rare bookshop in Manchester, where he was working, and had brought him home to catalog his libraries. Fifteen years later, DaShawn was the butler and manager of the Hall, Gerald could concentrate on his beloved horses, and Jessica did her work with a much brighter smile on her face.

Only twelve actual servants lived up at the house now, including the gardening staff. Cleaners came in every day that they were open to the public, and the stable was full of grooms and lads and jockeys all day, every day. But the main house was empty. Now that Gerald was gone, Patricia found herself looking forward to the added noise and bustle of the strangers who came to stare at her great-grandmother's portrait and the Elizabethan suit of armour.

"Yes, it was a bit of a bloodbath, wasn't it?"

"Blood swimming pool, if I may, ma'am."

"You may. If you'd just supported United over City..." and Patricia giggled at the swelling of DaShawn's dark brown cheeks.

"My lady does like her little jokes," he said with dignity.

"All right. I'm sorry. I'll be upstairs in a tick."

DaShawn, still offended by her idea, turned and left. People like DaShawn were why the Danbys had held onto this hall for seven hundred years. In more ways than one, she thought with a squirm. The fifth earl had had a controlling interest in a sugar plantation on Barbados. As in so much of the aristocracy, it was a chapter of their history that the docents didn't mention. Something else she would change.

Patricia dressed carefully. Not only for Daniel, who had in any case seen her in every state of dilapidated jackets and torn jodhpurs there was, but for the public, who slowly recognized her as she walked through them and down the hill to the stable. Her jodhpurs and boots were smart and she'd worn her newer working helmet, but her waxed jacket was loose on her and under it she wore a thick sweater against the cool damp the Birch Field often held on to even at the height of summer. She'd allowed extra time to be stopped and asked about the history of the house and grounds, but her picnic basket was weighing very heavy on her arm by the time she escaped into the courtyard.

Romany was already saddled and nickered at her happily when she saw her coming. Patricia went to her head first so she could feel the big muzzle root around against her coat, looking for horsenuts. She kissed Romany's star, fed her and looked around to find Daniel waiting patiently for her. A lad was holding Castle, his chestnut.

Starting as she meant to go on, Patricia smiled at him instead of giving him her usual supercilious nod. "Hello, Daniel."

"Hello," he said. "Let me take the basket."

Patricia gladly handed it over. The basket was designed with two articulating sections so that he could arrange it behind Castle's saddle. This he did in one smooth movement while Patricia allowed Romany to hunt out another horsenut or two.

When he had the basket arranged to his satisfaction, he looked back over to her. "Give you a hand up?" he asked politely, and for the first time in eight years.

"Thank you," she said evenly, though it was possible her cheeks had flushed enough for the curious onlookers to notice. She hoped her helmet hid any more blushes when Daniel bent beside her, took her knee and foot in his hands and tossed her onto Romany as though she weighed the same as the picnic basket. In moments he was also mounted and they were walking sedately out of the courtyard and southwest to the field.

Neither spoke. Patricia wondered if he was as full of memories as she. Also, she'd hoped she'd think of a way to open her speech before they arrived, but Romany was picking her way off the path and into the bumpy tussocks that signaled their arrival at the field before she'd found her words.

"Where to?" he said.

Well, *not* where they'd spent that night. The sprawling chestnut tree beyond the meadow beckoned her, but she turned her face and continued south to where the stream followed the curve of the road. Or rather, where the road followed the stream.

Not having to look at Daniel helped. "I looked into what you said," she called over her shoulder. "You're right. We can make the money if we sell these acres. Do you really think the village will be happy to have forty or fifty more houses on their doorstep?"

"Some'll complain. But not the shopkeepers or the farmers with their market stalls." His voice was coming and going on the wind that brought the loamy scent of the farmland beyond the road. "Harris over there'll get his bigger road, I reckon. He won't complain about that. He'll be able to bring bigger machinery in, get his fields harvested quicker."

"That's good."

He rode up beside her and they made their way down to the stream. She'd come this way with him before, even if not to this particular stretch of water. That day, awkward, unsure, knowing what she'd wanted but not how to get there, she'd meandered alongside him for what felt like miles before he'd put out a hand and said, "Tricia."

Her eyes were closed; she all but felt his hand on her cheek. But no. He was sitting on Castle, the fits of light coming through the thick summer canopy overhead turning Castle's coat gold and black. Leaves floated down the stream and the loamy, moldy smell, at once unpleasant and life-giving, filled her nostrils.

Romany was straining for the flowing water, so Patricia dismounted and let her step among the slippery rocks to take a drink. Daniel silently followed suit, so that for a moment they stood side by side, slack reins in hand, close enough to touch. He wore a buttondown shirt and tie under a jacket in a heathered check that put him right at home in the woods. Patricia looked down so she wouldn't ogle his shoulders, and so got to ogle his weathered old riding boots and tight-fitting jodhpurs instead.

"Won't do to have her drink too much," she said, or whispered.

"No."

Patricia gave a half-hearted tug on the reins, but Romany was well-trained and turned back to her, ready for instructions. The problem was, Patricia didn't have any. Her awareness of Daniel's body next to her was making her so heated she regretted the thick sweater, even though under the trees the air was cool.

"Will we eat Mrs. Gennaro's lunch?" Daniel said.

That sounded like enough of a plan to be going on with. "Yes. Let's not let it get cold. Or hot." She trusted Mrs. Gennaro's cooking and hadn't asked her for anything more specific than "a picnic."

Daniel mounted Castle and led the way back up the bank and she watched the paniers undulate with the horse's step, and Daniel's straight back in front of them. She'd tried Western riding on one of her trips to America, and she could see its charms (and those of its cowboys), but nothing could compare to the shoulders of a man who was holding his reins in both hands and posting a trot like he was born to an English saddle. Which Daniel wasn't, but he might as well have been. Generations back, before the mining and factory work that had defined his family, one of Daniel's ancestors must have known horses.

They burst into the sunlight and Patricia's need to squint made her lose sight of him for a moment. He aimed for the lone chestnut tree that stood to their left, whose heavy branches would protect Patricia's skin from the sun, though it was the one place she'd told herself she wouldn't go. In silence, they dismounted and tied the horses to a low branch, then emptied the basket of its delicacies.

Mrs. Gennaro had provided sandwiches with thick slices of ham and tomato or roast chicken and stuffing, scotch eggs, fingers of cucumber and carrot, sturdy jam tarts with Patricia's favourite blackcurrant jam, chocolate chip cookies (what had Mrs. Gennaro heard? Perhaps Patricia was reading too much into them) and, of course, strawberries. She'd also tucked a half-bottle of pinot grigio and two plastic wineglasses into the paniers along with two small bottles of water. It was a simple lunch, but there was so much food Patricia began to laugh. "Does she think we're going to be here for the night?"

Daniel's eyes met hers. Okay, bad choice of words. Patricia blushed. Why did it have to be *this* piece of land that Daniel wanted her to sell? Why did she have to invite him to it at all? She could have had this conversation in his office.

Where she'd had that other one, that had gone so well the other day.

Yes, so. Birch Field it was. She poured them both wine and to the sound of the two horses scronching happily at the grass, they sat on the mossier ground under the tree.

"I forgot a blanket," she said.

"A wet bum'll do you no harm for a bit." The ground wasn't wet, exactly, but the moss held moisture. Still, she was damned if she was going to distract herself, now they were here.

To eat or not to eat first? Daniel held out the container holding the chicken and stuffing sandwiches. He knew they were her favourite. She took one, but instead of bringing it to her mouth, she said in a rush, "Do you think you'll go to America?"

He put down the ham and tomato he'd been about to bite into. Without her helmet on, she had no way to hide from his dark stare. "Do you think you'll sell the horses to Hamid?"

"I..." She should say no, not in a million years. Not because Hamid wouldn't take care of them, but because Daniel had given her an alternative. But if the horses didn't go, Daniel wouldn't be able to go with them to the best job of his career. "It's a fantastic opportunity."

"Aye. You said that."

She lowered her head and bit into her food, just to have something to do. The scent of thyme almost distracted her, but not quite. She swallowed. "Yes. Well, it is. But you know that." Okay, could this piece of food in her throat go down now? She felt like a bird who'd swallowed a gerbil.

"Y'all right?" he asked, and there they were again. The memories were not going to let her alone.

"I'm sorry, Daniel," she said, screwing her courage to the sticking place. It didn't matter what order it came out in, as long as she said it. "I'm sorry about that night. And all the nights since."

His gaze had sharpened, his eyes narrowing so they were sparks of light. "What night?"

"The carol singing. I... I wish I'd...found you later. Apologized. I wish I'd swung at Bernard and interrupted the whole thing and told him to go home, and hang if my father heard. I wish I'd had the courage to be who you'd believed I was. And in all the years since then, I've allowed myself to be cross with you because you've reacted to me as anyone would, after thinking I'd rejected you that way. I'm sorry that I didn't write, that I couldn't find words to tell you what that night had meant to me. The other night, I mean." She looked around at the field, at the memory.

He could have blistered her skin with the intensity of his eyes. "What *did* it meant to you?"

She had to be careful. But she had to be truthful. She shook her head as if shaking her hair out of her face, though today she wore it in a fat plait.

"Back then?" she said, meeting his eyes. "Everything."

Her wine glass was no longer in her hands. Daniel was leaning toward her, filling her vision. His lips barely moved when he said, "And now?"

Was she staring at his lips? They were so close. As close as they'd been in Gerald's study the day of the funeral. He wasn't the only man she'd ever kissed, but he was the most important.

Yet she couldn't say it. She had to focus on the reason she'd brought him here. "What I'm trying to say," she answered instead, "is that I put the burden of...of sanctifying that memory, of turning that night into a fairy tale I hadn't wanted to wake from, on you, and when I was naïve and scared and hurt your feelings, I was too young and stupid to know how to walk it back. And I was your employer, however much you worked for Dad rather than me, and I played on that power to keep you annoyed but in front of me. And I'm sorry for that."

Daniel hadn't moved. She didn't know how she'd gotten all the words out, but there seemed too many of them now, and they disintegrated on the heated air between the two of them.

"That's not what I asked," he said, his voice so low she could feel it through the ground. "What does it mean to you?" He put one hand to her cheek, traced her ear. "What does it mean now?"

She was bewitched, spellbound, ruined. "Everything," she breathed, and Daniel kissed her.

It was just the same. He was the same, but so much better, because she was older and knew that the rush of blood to her head, to her hands, to everywhere, was something she'd never felt with anyone else the way she'd felt it with him. That her sigh of relief, of thanks, was for a feeling that she hadn't felt in eight years. That love could be as uncomplicated as she liked, if she remembered that she was just Tricia, a young lass from York-shire, who got to be held in the strong arms of the man she loved.

His arms tightened on her back and Patricia wriggled closer, half-reclining so she could lift her face and deepen the kiss. She brought her hand up to run it through his black hair, to hold him to her, to taste his lips with her tongue and encourage him to open his mouth so she could taste him more thoroughly.

Daniel broke off the kiss. Drugged, her eyelids heavy, Patricia looked at him. His lips were wet from hers. His hair had fallen over his forehead. Two spots of colour were on his cheeks. "Tricia," he said, his voice ragged.

"That's right," she smiled, not letting go of his head. "Kiss me again."

So he did, and for several blissful moments she knew nothing else.

Thought only reappeared gradually. *Mine,* she thought first. *Mine. I earned him. I saw him first. He's mine.* Then, *He's done everything for us and never asked for anything in return.*

He loves the land like I do. The horses more, but the land because it sustains the horses. Because it has sustained us.

He loves the horses.

He could take them all to America.

He should take them.

I can't ask him to stay here.

She broke away, fast, so fast that Daniel almost dropped her, his hands sliding away from her back. She braced herself with one hand under her. Her wet lips cooled in the breeze, making her shiver.

"What is it?" he said, not backing up.

How much did she love him? He'd earned more than just her company for the rest of his life. He'd earned freedom, riches, recognition.

Patricia stood. "You have to take Hamid's offer."

Daniel followed her warily. "What?"

"Take Hamid's offer. Go to America. Make millions." She'd found her helmet and was clipping it under her chin.

"What are you talking about?"

"I'm saying," she said, straining for a voice of reason, of calm certainty, "that you must go. You have no reason to stay. I'm saying, please go. With my blessing. And Gerald's. And all of us."

She went over to Romany and retightened her cinch, then began untying her from the tree. But her hands were clumsy, shaking with her effort.

"Tricia, what—"

"It's all right, Daniel." She got the reins free at last, swung herself up onto the horse. "You can take the horses. Gerald would be happy to know you—"

She couldn't say any more. Her throat closed over, seeing him standing in the meadow, the grass that belonged to the land that she loved so much reaching his knees, seeming to hold him to itself. She had to send him away. So she clicked her tongue and set Romany at a brisk walk that quickly turned into a canter when she reached the path, leaving Daniel staring after her, the afternoon sun burnishing his hair auburn.

Patricia set Romany to a gallop for the few hundred yards of straight run, just to have a reason not to think, to avoid tree branches and keep an eye out for animals. To tire out her thighs from the unaccustomed crouch she held over the saddle. She'd spent so many years avoiding Daniel, when she wasn't flipping her tail in front of him. So much wasted effort. And now her clarity was only breaking her heart.

She slowed to a canter when she came to the paddock fencing by the stable, and hoped that she wouldn't attract too much attention as she approached the yard, trying to stabilize her breathing, blinking the tears away.

Romany walked happily into the yard, blowing hard, looking forward to a drink and a brush-down. No one approached them at first. Patricia dismounted and stood for a moment, looking around her, leaning on Romany's shoulder.

Three sides of a rectangle made up the stable blocks, most with big gentle heads looking over their doors, greeting Romany with the odd nicker. Fresh green paint adorned all the half-doors Patricia could see. The rest of the yard was made up of clean whitewashed wood. Daniel had a rota system that kept the dust off everything so even the windows of his office shone.

Crackerjax walked past her, led by one of the lads. By Jackie Eau out of Roundtree Chanticleer, she had begun to win races since Ascot, one of the many success stories Gerald and Daniel had achieved between them. She was perfect: slender legs, muscular haunches, a proud head and an efficient movement even at a walk.

"Want me to take Romany when I get Crackerjax in her stall, my lady?" the lad asked. But

Patricia didn't answer him. She was looking at another lad, backing into the far side of the yard with a Jeep full of hay. Four other workers began to attack the load, carrying it to the feedcages next to each horse's head. More nickering and blowing from the contented and hungry horses.

"My lady?" said the groom.

Patricia listened. The afternoon was quiet, yet the sounds of her life were everywhere. Clinking of harnesses. Water being sprayed on a horse's legs after a ride. Birds flying and chirping everywhere, stealing hay for their own homes in the eaves. Lads murmuring just out of range, laughing with each other while they worked. The grumble of the Jeep, and its accompanying smell of diesel, an unavoidable addition to any stable's atmosphere.

Daniel cantered into the yard at that moment, forestalling the groom's repetition of his question. He came to a halt right next to Romany, whose head reared at the sudden arrival, almost pulling the reins out of Patricia's nerveless hands. Daniel swung his left leg forward and over Castle's back so he landed on two feet, facing Patricia.

"You can't just ride away like that," he began, tempering his voice so it wouldn't carry to the curious onlookers. "You can't just say what you said and—"

"I lied," she interrupted, and only when she tasted her tears did she realize she was crying. "I don't want you to go. If you leave, I won't be able to keep going."

There was a beat while he took in what she said. Then, "I'm not going anywhere," he growled, and folded her in his arms.

Patricia hid her face in his neck and felt her shoulders shake. But only for a moment, because he held her away from him then, shook his head, said, "Hey, lass."

"I'm so selfish," she cried. "I tried to let you go. I can't give you what he can. But I want you to stay with me anyway. Keep the horses here."

"They belong here," he said.

"Yes!" She was being loud, and knew that they were surrounded now by grooms and lads and who knew who else, but she couldn't care. She was talking and sobbing at the same time. "I couldn't face going through my day without knowing that you're down here, or riding on the downs, or...just walking, just being. I'll sell the Birch Field. I'll sell half the estate if it means you and the horses will stay."

Daniel's face was softer than she'd ever seen it, a small smile of incredulity and peace on his lips. "We're staying." He cupped her face in his hands. "If it were you and me and a bedsit in Middlesbrough, we'd still be you and me, lass, and that's all I want."

Patricia laughed through her tears, and was still smiling when he kissed her and the surrounding crowd serenaded them with cheers and wolf whistles.

THE END

Other Books by Kimberley Ash

The Fieldings:
Breathe
Hold
Stand
Rise
Available now from Tea Rose Publishing.

The Van Allen Brothers:
Forgive Me
Forget Me
Free Me
Available now from Tule Publishing.

Connect with Kimberley

I really hope you enjoyed reading *Champion* as much as I enjoyed writing it! Please let me know if you would like to see more modern regency romance via any and all of my social media accounts. Join my Facebook Group, Read Your Ash Off, sign up for my newsletter, and follow me to get the latest info on my new releases and events. I look forward to meeting you!

Website: www.kimberleyash.com

Bookbub: @KimberleyAsh

Instagram: @KAshAuthor

Goodreads: Kimberley Ash

Pinterest: @KAshAuthor

Facebook Page: Kimberley Ash Books

About the Author

As a teen, Kimberley Ash would sit in her boarding school dormitory and read Silhouette Romances with her friends. They would have passionate arguments about the kind of American hero they really wanted to see in the books, so to settle things, Kimberley wrote one. While she took great pleasure in deconstructing alpha males and exposing their chiseled but vulnerable underbellies, life and inner demons made her put away her dreams for twenty-five years. She was forty before she realized that what she wanted to be when she grew up was what she'd always wanted to be: a romance writer. So she joined New Jersey Romance Writers, took all the classes she could find, and has never looked back. Her first novel, *Breathe*, was published in 2018. She has since published the Van Allen Brothers series with Tule Publishing (2019) and the Fieldings series (2022-23), which includes sequels to *Breathe*.

Meanwhile, to her great surprise, Kimberley was swept off her feet by her own all-American hero. Now making her home in rural New Jersey (yes, there is a rural New Jersey) with him, two hybrid children and two big furry dogs, she can be found staring into a computer screen, wrestling with plotlines and ignoring the giant dustbunnies.

Kimberley holds a bachelor's degree in French from Queen Mary College (spectacularly useful at PTA meetings) and a master's in English Literature from Drew University (NJ).

Kimberley writes about real life and therefore celebrates and supports diversity in all its forms. You can find her obsessing about tea on Facebook, Instagram, and Threads.